I0669192

Reprint Publishing

FOR PEOPLE WHO GO FOR ORIGINALS.

www.reprintpublishing.com

"Simple enough; I've stopped the clock," he said.—Page 132.—*Frontispiece*.

MOLLIE AND THE UNWISEMAN

BY JOHN KENDRICK BANGS

Illustrations by
ALBERT LEVERING and
CLARE VICTOR DWIGGINS.

Henry T. Coates & Co.,
Philadelphia.

CONTENTS.

LIST OF FULL-PAGE ILLUSTRATIONS.

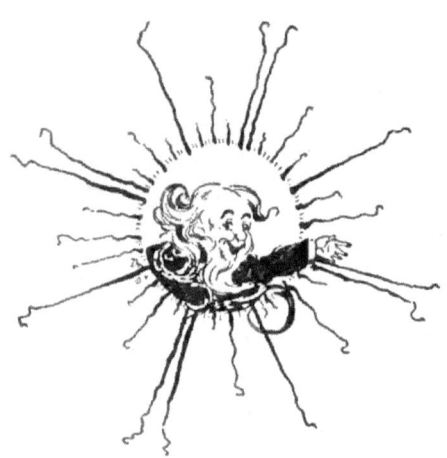

I
BOPEEP

In which Mollie meets the Unwiseman

MOLLIE had been romping in the hay all the afternoon. With her were Flaxilocks, the French doll, and young Whistlebinkie, the rubber boy, who had got his name from the fact that he had a whistle set in the top of his beaver hat. Flaxilocks and Whistlebinkie could stand a great deal of romping, and so also could Mollie, but, on the whole, the little girl was not so strong as the dolls were, and in consequence

7

along above five o'clock, having settled herself down comfortably on the shaded side of
the haystack, a great pillow of sweet-scented
clover grass under her head, it is not to be
wondered at that Mollie should begin to
ponder. Now it is a curious thing, but
Mollie always has singular adventures when
she ponders. Things happen to her then
which happen at no other times, and which
also, as far as I have been able to find out,
never happen to other little girls.

It was this way upon this particular afternoon, as you will see when you read on.
She had been pondering for three or four
minutes when almost directly at her side she
heard a sob.

" Who's that ?" she asked, sleepily, gazing
around her.

" Who's what ?" said Flaxilocks, sitting
up and opening her great blue eyes so suddenly that something inside of her head
seemed to click.

"Somebody's sobbing," said Mollie.

"Somebody's sobbing," said Mollie.

"I guess not," returned Flaxilocks. "We are all alone here. Nobody could have sobbed unless it was Whistlebinkie. Whistlebinkie, did you sob?"

"No," said Whistlebinkie, "'twasn't me. I can't sob because I haven't got a sobber to sob with. I've only got a whistle."

"Maybe I dreamed it," said Mollie, apparently satisfied for the moment, and then the three threw themselves back on the hay once more and began their pondering anew.

They did not ponder very long, however, for in a few moments Flaxilocks rose up again and observed:

"I heard a sob myself just now, Mollie."

"So-*di*," whistled Whistlebinkie, through the top of his hat.

"Whistlebinkie," said Mollie, severely, "how often must I tell you not to talk through your hat, but through your mouth? So-*di* doesn't mean anything. It isn't English. If you will only remember to use your hat to whistle through and your mouth for conversation every one will be able to understand. What do you mean by So-*di*?"

"So—did—I," said Whistlebinkie, meekly, this time using his mouth as Mollie had instructed him to do.

"Then you heard the sob?"

"Yes—ma'am—plain—as—can—be," returned Whistlebinkie.

"And no wonder," observed Flaxilocks, pointing one of her kid fingers off to her left. "Why shouldn't we all hear a sob when there is a poor little maid weeping so near at hand?"

"So there is," said Mollie, looking toward the spot at which Flaxilocks was pointing, where there sat a pretty little shepherdess with tears streaming down her cheeks. "Isn't it queer?"

"Very," said Whistlebinkie. "Shall I give a whistle of surprise, ma'am?"

"No," said Mollie. "I'm not surprised enough for that."

Then she got up and walked over to the strange little girl's side, and taking her hand in hers asked her softly why she wept.

"I'm little Bopeep," said the stranger. "And I've lost my sheep, and I don't know where to find them."

"Oh, is that all?" asked Mollie.

"Isn't it enough?" returned Bopeep, gazing with surprise at Mollie through her tears. "They were all spring lambs and I'm very much afraid some hungry man may have stolen them away and drowned them in the mint sauce pond."

"Dear me, how dreadful!" cried Mollie.

"Shall I give a whistle of terror, ma'am?" asked Whistlebinkie.

"No, don't," said Flaxilocks. "Save your breath. We ought to help Bopeep to find her flock."

"That's so," said Mollie. "Would you like to have us do that, Bopeep?"

"Oh, it would be very sweet of you if you

would," sobbed the little shepherdess. "I can't tell you how glad I'd be."

"I'll whistle it for you if you want me to," said the obliging Whistlebinkie, which, as

"I'll whistle it for you."

no one objected, he immediately proceeded to do. When he had finished Bopeep thanked him, and asked him if he were any relation to her old friend Flutiboy who was the only person she knew who could whistle as charmingly as he, which pleased Whistle-binkie very much because he had heard of the famous Flutiboy, and was well aware that he was the champion whistler of the world.

"Now let us be off to find the sheep," said Mollie. "Which way did they go, Bopeep?"

"They went every way," said Bopeep, her eyes filling with tears again.

"I don't see how that could be," said Flaxilocks, "unless one quarter of lamb went one way, and another another, and so on."

"Oh, it was easy enough for them," said Bopeep. "There were four of them, and one went north, one south, one east, and one west. If they had all run off together I could have run away with them, but as it was all I could do was stand still and let them go. I love them all equally, and since

14

I couldn't favor any special one, or divide myself up into four parts, I had to let them go."

" Perflyawfle," whistled Whistlebinkie through his hat.

"Whistlebinkie!" cried Mollie, reprovingly.

" Puf-fick-ly or-full," said Whistlebinkie distinctly through his little red rubber teeth.

"Well, I say we keep together in looking for them, anyhow," said Flaxilocks. " Because it's bad enough to lose the sheep without losing ourselves, and it seems to me there being four of us we can find the first sheep four times as quickly if we stick together as we could if we went alone; and that of course means that we'll find the four sheep sixteen times as quickly as we would if we went alone."

" I don't quite see that," said Bopeep.

" It's plain enough," observed Flaxilocks. " Four times four is sixteen."

"Oh, yes," said Bopeep. "I see."

"Sodwi," whistled Whistlebinkie. "I mean so—do—I," he added quickly, as he noted Mollie's frown.

So the four little folk started off in search of the missing sheep, Whistlebinkie and Flaxilocks running on ahead, and Mollie and Bopeep with their arms lovingly about each other bringing up in the rear.

"Did you ever lose the sheep before, Bopeep?" asked Mollie, after they had walked a little way in silence.

"Oh my, yes," returned Bopeep. "I'm losing them all the time. It is a part of my duty to lose them. If I didn't, you know, the nursery rhyme couldn't go on."

"And you always find them again?" Mollie put in.

"Always. That's got to happen, too. If they didn't come back and bring their tails behind them the nursery rhyme would be spoiled again."

16

"Then I don't see why you feel so badly about it," said Mollie.

"I have to," replied Bopeep. "That's part of my business, too. I sometimes wish old Mother Goose hadn't employed me to look after the sheep at all, because it keeps me crying all the time, and I don't find crying very pleas- ant. Why, do you know, I have

"And I only get five cents a quart."

been in this sheep-losing business for nearly

17

two hundred years now, and I've cried about seventy gallons of tears every year. Just think of that. That means fourteen thousand gallons of tears, and I only get five cents a quart, which doesn't more than pay my dressmaker's bills. I asked my employers some years ago to let me have an assistant to do the crying for me, but they wouldn't do it, which I think was very mean, don't you?"

"Yes, I do," said Mollie. "I should think just losing the sheep was hard enough work for a little girl like you to attend to."

"That's what I think—but dear me, where are Whistlebinkie and Flaxilocks going?" said Bopeep. "They mustn't go that way. The first place we must go to is the home of the Unwiseman."

"The what?" demanded Mollie.

"The Unwiseman. He's an unwiseman who doesn't know anything," explained Bopeep. "The rules require that we go to him first and ask him if he knows where the sheep are. He'll say he doesn't know, and then we'll go on to the little old woman who lives under the hill. She'll know where they are, but she'll tell us wrong. Hi! Whistlebinkie and Flaxilocks! Turn off to the left, and stop at that little red house under the oak tree."

"There isn't any little red house under the oak tree," said Mollie.

"Oh, yes, there is," said Bopeep. "Only you've got to know it's there before you can see it. The Unwiseman lives there."

Whistlebinkie and Flaxilocks did as they were told, and, sure enough, in a minute there appeared a little red house under the oak tree just as Bopeep had said. Mollie was delighted, it was such a dainty little house, with its funny gables and a roof made of strawberry icing. The window-panes were shining like silver, and if Bopeep was not mistaken were made of sugar.

But funnier still was the Unwiseman him-self, a queer-looking, wrinkled-up little old man who sat in the doorway trying to smoke a pipe filled with soapsuds.

"Good-afternoon, O Unwiseman," said Bopeep.

"Hoh!" sneered the Unwiseman. "Good-afternoon! This isn't afternoon. It's day before yesterday morning."

Mollie giggled.

"Hush!" whispered Bopeep. "He doesn't know any better. You can see that he doesn't know anything by looking at his pipe. He's been trying to smoke those soapsuds now for a week. The week before he was trying to blow bubbles with it, only he had corn-silk in it then instead of soapsuds. That shows what kind of a man he is."

"What can I do for you to-day, Bopeep?" asked the Unwiseman as he touched a lighted match to the suds, which imme-diately sputtered and went out.

"I wanted to know if you had seen any- thing of my sheep," said Bo- peep. "Let's see," said the Unwise- man. "Let's see Sheep are what? They aren't anything like tele- graph poles

Sat in the doorway trying to smoke a pipe filled with soapsuds.

or wheelbarrows, are they?"

"No," said Bopeep, "they are not."

"Then maybe I have seen them," said the Unwiseman, with a smile of satisfaction. "Maybe I have. Several things went by here day after to-morrow that weren't a bit like wheelbarrows or telegraph poles. They may have been your sheep. One of the things had four red wheels on it—have any of your sheep got four red wheels on them?"

"They aren't anything like telegraph poles or wheelbarrows, are they?"

Whistlebinkie nearly exploded as the Unwiseman said this, but the queer old gentleman was not learned enough to know mirth when he saw it, so that no harm was done.

22

"No," said Bopeep. "My sheep had no wheels."

"Then I must have seen them," said the Unwiseman. "There was a thing went by here a week from next Tuesday noon that hadn't any wheels. It had two legs and carried a fan, or a fish-pole—I couldn't tell which it was—and it was whistling. Maybe that was one of the sheep."

"No," said Bopeep again, shaking her head. "My sheep don't whistle and they have four legs."

"Nonsense," said the Unwiseman, with a wink. "You can't fool me that way. I know a horse when I hear one described, and when any one tells me that the thing with four legs and no whistle is a sheep I know better. And so my dear, since you've tried to trifle with me you can go along. I won't tell you another thing about your old sheep. I don't know anything about 'em anyhow."

Whereupon the old man got up from his chair and climbed the oak tree to look for apples, while the searching party went on to the little old woman who lived under the hill, and Bopeep asked her if she knew

anything about the sheep.

"Yes," said the little old woman, with a frown which frightened poor Whistlebinkie so that he gasped and whistled softly in spite of his efforts

"One of 'em's gone to the moon."

to keep quiet. "Yes,

24

I've seen your sheep. I know just where they are, too. One of 'em's gone to the moon. Another has been adopted by a girl named Mary, who is going to take it to school and make the children laugh. Another has sold his wool to a city merchant, and the fourth has accepted an invitation to dinner from a member of Congress. He will reach the dinner at half-past seven to-night on a silver platter. He will be decorated with green peas and mint sauce. Now get along with you."

Mollie felt very sorry for poor Bopeep as she listened to this dreadful statement, and she was very much surprised to see Bopeep smiling through it all.

"Why did you smile?" she asked the little shepherdess as they wended their way home again.

"Because I knew from what she said that she knew the sheep were safe—but she lives on ink, and that makes her disagreeable.

25

She just wanted to make me feel as disagreeable as she does, and she told me
all that nonsense to accomplish that purpose."

"The horrid thing!" said Mollie.

"No," said Bo-
peep. "She isn't
really horrid. It's
only because she
lives on ink that
she seems
so. Sup-
pose you
had to
live on
ink?"

"I'd

be horrid, too,"
said Mollie.

"She lives on ink and it makes her
disagreeable."

"There they are!" cried Bopeep joyfully,
and sure enough there were the sheep, and
they had brought their tails behind them,

26

too. They were grazing close beside the hay-stack on which Mollie had been pondering.

"I am very much obliged to you for your help and company," said Bopeep, "and now as it is six o'clock, I must drive my sheep home. Good-by."

"Good-by," said Mollie, kissing the little shepherdess affectionately.

"Good-by," said Flaxilocks, sinking back on the clover pillow, and closing her great blue eyes again.

"Gubby," whistled Whistlebinkie through his hat.

"Wasn't it queer?" said Mollie later as they wended their way home again.

"Very," said Flaxilocks.

"Queeresperiensieverad," whistled Whistlebinkie.

"What's that?" cried Mollie.

"Queerest—experience—I—ever—had," said Whistlebinkie.

"Ah!" said Mollie. "I didn't care much for the little old woman under the hill, but that funny old Unwiseman—I'd like to meet him again."

And the others agreed that it would indeed be pleasant to do so.

A Visit to the Unwiseman. II

In which Mollie renews an acquaintance

"Whistlebinkie," said Mollie, one afternoon, as she and he were swaying gently to and fro in the hammock, "do you remember the little red house under the oak tree?"

"Yessum," whistled Whistlebinkie, "I mean yes—ma'am," he added hurriedly.

"And the Unwiseman who lived there?"

"Yes, I remember him puffickly," said Whistlebinkie. "I think he knows less than any person I ever sawed."

"Not sawed but saw, Whistlebinkie," said

Mollie, who was very anxious that her rubber doll should speak correctly.

"Oh, yes!" cried Whistlebinkie. "I think he sawed less than any man I ever knew— or rather—well—I guess you know what I mean, don't you?"

"Yes, I do," said Mollie, with a smile. "But tell me, Whistlebinkie dear, wouldn't you like to go with me, and pay the Unwiseman a visit?"

"Has he sent you a bill?" asked Whistlebinkie.

"What for, pray?" queried Mollie, with a glance of surprise at Whistlebinkie.

"To tell you that you owed him a visit, of course," said Whistlebinkie. "There isn't any use of our paying him anything unless we owe him something, is there?"

"Oh, I see!" said Mollie. "No, we don't owe him one, but I think we'd enjoy ourselves very much if we made him one."

"All right, let's," said Whistlebinkie.

"What'll we make it of, worsted or pasteboard?"

"Whistlebinkie," observed Mollie, severely, "you are almost as absurd as the old man himself. The idea of making a visit out of worsted or pasteboard! Come along. Stop your joking and let us start."

The rubber doll was quite willing to agree to this, and

A pasteboard visit.

off they started. In a very little while they were down under the spreading branches of the great oak tree, but, singular to relate, the little red house that had stood there the last time they had called was not to be seen.

"Dear me!" cried Mollie, "what can have become of it, do you suppose, Whistlebinkie?"

"I give it up," said the rubber doll,

31

scratching his hat so that he could think more easily. "Haven't an idea—unless the old man discovered that its roof was made of strawberry icing, and ate it up."

"Ho! Ho! Ho!" laughed some one from behind them.

Mollie and Whistlebinkie turned quickly, and lo and behold, directly behind them stood the little Unwiseman himself, trying to dig the oak tree up by the roots with a small teaspoon he held in his hand.

"The idea of my eating up my house! Hoh! What nonsense. Hoh!" he said, as the visitors turned.

"Well, what has become of it, then?" asked Mollie.

"I've moved it, that's what," said the Unwiseman. "I couldn't get any apples on this oak tree, so I moved my house over under the willow tree down by the brook."

"But you can't get apples on a willow tree, either, can you?" asked Mollie.

"I don't know yet," said the Unwiseman. "I haven't lived there long enough to find out, but I can try, and that's all anybody can do."

"And what are you doing

with that teaspoon?" asked Whistle-binkie.

"You see, I don't want to swallow an acorn and have a great big tree like that grow up in me."

3   33

"I'm digging up this oak tree," said the Unwiseman. "I want to get the acorn it grew out of. I'm very fond of acorns, but I'm afraid to eat them, unless the tree that's in 'em has grown out. You see, I don't want to swallow an acorn, and have a great big tree like that grow up in me. It wouldn't be comfortable."

Whistlebinkie said he thought that was a very good idea, because there could not be any doubt that it would be extremely awkward for any man, wise or unwise, to have an oak tree sprouting up inside of him.

"What are you so anxious to know about my house for?" asked the Unwiseman, suddenly stopping short in his work with the teaspoon. "You don't want to rent it for the summer, do you?"

"Whistlebinkie and I have come down to call upon you, that's all," explained Mollie.

"Well now, really?" said the Unwiseman, rising, and dropping the teaspoon. "That's too bad, isn't it? Here you've come all this way to see me and I am out. I shall be *so* disappointed when I get home and find that you have been there and I not there to see you. Dear! Dear! How full of disappointments t h i s world is. You couldn't come again last night, could you? I was home then."

"Not very well," said Whistlebinkie. "Mollie's father doesn't like it if we turn the clock back."

"D e a r m e! That's too bad, too! My!" said

Turning the clock back.

the old fellow, with a look of real sadness on his face. "What a disappointment, to be sure. You call and find me out! I *do* wish there was some way to arrange it, so that I might be at home when you call. You can't think of any, can you, Miss Whistlebinkie?"

"Perhaps now that you know we are coming," said Mollie, who, while her last name was *not* Whistlebinkie, did not think it necessary to pay any attention to the old man's mistake, which amused her very much, "perhaps now that you know we are coming you might run ahead and be there when we arrive."

"That's the scheme!" said Whistlebinkie.

"Yes, that's a first-rate plan," said the old man, nodding his head. "There's only one thing against it, perhaps."

"What's that?" asked Whistlebinkie.

"That I don't know," replied the Unwiseman, "which is very unfortunate, because it may be serious. For instance, suppose the objection should turn out to be in the shape of a policeman, who had a warrant to arrest me for throwing stones at somebody's pet tiger. What could I do?"

"But you haven't been throwing stones at anybody's pet tiger, have you?" asked Mollie.

"Not while I was awake," said the Unwiseman. "But I may have done it in my sleep, you know. People do lots of things in their sleep that they never do while awake.

"Not while I was awake, but I may have done it in my sleep, you know."

They snore, for instance; and one man I know, who always rides when he is awake, walks in his sleep."

37

"Let's try it, anyway," said Whistlebinkie.
"It may be that there won't be any trouble,
after all."

"Very well," assented the Unwiseman.
"I'm willing if you are, only if I am arrested
it will be all your fault, and you must promise to tell the policeman that it was you who
threw the stones at the tiger and not I."

Mollie and Whistlebinkie feeling sure that
nothing of the kind would happen, readily
made the promise, and the queer little old
man started off for his house as fast as his
legs could carry him.

The two small visitors followed slowly,
and in a few minutes had reached the
Unwiseman's door down by the willow
tree. The door was tightly closed, so they
knocked. For a while there was no answer,
and then they knocked again. In response
to this they heard a shuffling step within,
and a voice which they recognized as that
of the Unwiseman called out:

38

"Is that a policeman? Because if it is, I'm not at home. I went out three weeks ago and won't be back again for six years, and, furthermore, I never threw stones at a pet tiger in my life unless I was asleep, and that don't count."

"We aren't police-men," said Mollie. "We're Mollie and Whistlebinkie come to see you."

"Oh, indeed!" cried

"Is that a policeman?"

the Unwiseman from within, as he threw the door open wide. "Why, what a pleasant surprise! I had no idea you were coming. Walk right in. So glad to see you."

Whistlebinkie giggled slightly through his beaver hat as he and Mollie, accepting the invitation, walked in and seated themselves

39

in a droll little parlor that opened on the left-hand side of the hall.

"So this is your house, is it?" said Mollie, glancing about her with much interest.

"Yes," said the Unwiseman; "but, Miss Whistlebinkie, won't you kindly sit on the table instead of on that chair? So many people have been hurt by chairs breaking under them—many times more than are hurt from sitting on tables—that I have to be very careful. I have no doubt the chairs are strong enough to hold you, but I don't want to take any chances. I think it will rain next year, don't you?" he added. "And you haven't brought any umbrellas! Too bad, too bad. If you should get wet, you'd find it very damp. Really, you ought never to go out without an umbrella. I always do, but then I know enough to go in when it rains, so of course don't need one."

"I see you have a piano," said Whistlebinkie, taking in the furniture of the parlor.

40

"Yes," replied the Unwiseman. "It's a very fine one, too. It has lots of tunes locked up in it."

"Are you fond of music?" asked Mollie.

"No, I hate it,"

said the Unwiseman. "That's why I have the piano. There's just so much less music in the world. Nobody can get at the keys of that piano,

"Are you fond of music?" asked Mollie. "No, I hate it," said the Unwiseman.

so you see it's never played, which pleases me very much. If I were rich enough, I'd buy all the pianos, and organs, and fiddles, and horns, and drums in the world, and I'd keep 'em all locked up so that there never would be any more music at all."

41

"I am sorry to hear that," said Mollie. "I love music."

"Well," said the old man, generously, "you can have my share. Whenever anybody brings any music around where I am hereafter, I'll do it up in a package, and send it to you." "Thank you very much," said Mollie. "It's very good of you."

"Oh, it's no favor to you, I am sure!" put in the Unwiseman, hastily. "In fact, it's the other way. I'm obliged to you for taking it off my hands. If you want to you can open the piano right away, and take out all the tunes there are in it. I'll go off on the mountains while you are doing it, so that it won't annoy me any."

"Oh, no!" said Mollie. "I'd a great deal rather have you to talk to than all the tunes in the piano."

"Very well," said the old man, with a smile of pleasure. "What shall we talk about, frogs?"

"I don't know anything about frogs," said Mollie.

"Neither do I," returned the Unwiseman. "I don't know the difference between a frog and a watch-chain, except that one chains watches and the other doesn't, but which does and which doesn't I haven't a notion."

"I see you have all your pictures with their faces turned to the wall," said Mollie, looking about the room again so as to avoid laughing in the Unwiseman's face. "What is that for?"

"That's to make them more interesting," replied the Unwiseman. "They're a very uninteresting lot of pictures, and I never could get anybody to look at 'em until I turned them hind side before, that way. Now everybody wants to see them."

Mollie rose up, and turned one of them about so that she could see it.

"It's very pretty," she said. "What is it a picture of—a meadow?"

43

"No. It's a picture of me," said the Un-wiseman. "And it's one of the best I ever had taken."

"But I don't see you in it," said Mollie. "All I can see is a great field of grass and a big bowlder down in one corner."

"I know it," said the Un-wiseman. "I'm lying on my back be-hind the bowl-der asleep. If

"It's a picture of me."

you could move the bowlder you could see me, but you can't. It's too heavy, and, besides, I think the paint is glued on."

"I hope you don't lie on the ground asleep very much," said Mollie, gravely, for

44

she had taken a great liking to this strange old man who didn't know anything. "You might catch your death of cold."

"I didn't say I was lying on the ground," said the Unwiseman. "I said I was lying on my back. People ought not to catch cold lying on a nice warm back like mine."

"And do you live here all alone?" asked Mollie.

"Yes, I don't need anybody to live with. Other people know things, and it always makes them proud, and I don't like proud people."

"I hope you like me," said Mollie, softly.

"Yes, indeed, I do," cried the Unwiseman. "I like you and Whistlebinkie very much, because you don't either of you know any-thing either, and so, of course, you aren't stuck up like some people I meet who think just because they know the difference be-tween a polar bear and a fog horn while I don't that they're so much better than I am.

45

I like you, and I hope you will come and see me again."

"I will, truly," said Mollie.

"Very well—and that you may get back sooner you'd better run right home now. It is getting late, and, besides, I have an engagement."

"You?" asked Mollie. "What with?"

"Well, don't you tell anybody," said the Unwiseman; "but I'm going up to the village to the drug store. I promised to meet myself up there at six o'clock, and it's quarter past now, so I must hurry."

"But what on earth are you going to do there?" asked Mollie.

"I'm going to buy myself a beaver hat just like Whistlebinkie's," returned the Unwiseman, gleefully, "I've got to have something to keep my tablecloth in, and a beaver hat strikes me as just the thing."

Saying which the Unwiseman bowed Mollie and Whistlebinkie out, and sped off like

The unwiseman sped off like lightning to the village drug store.—Page 46.

lightning in the direction of the village drug store, but whether or not he succeeded in getting a beaver hat there I don't know, for he never told me.

III

IN THE HOUSE OF THE UNWISEMAN

In which Mollie reads some strange rules

A FEW days later Mollie and Whistle-binkie were strolling together through the meadows when most unexpectedly they came upon the little red house of the Unwiseman.

"Why, I thought this house was under the willow tree," said Mollie.

"Sotwuz," whistled Whistlebinkie through his hat.

"What are you trying to say, Whistle-binkie?" asked Mollie.

"So — it — was," replied Whistlebinkie. "He must have moved it."

"But this isn't half as nice a place for it as the old one," said Mollie. "There isn't any shade here at all. Let's knock at the door, and see if he is at home. Maybe he will tell us why he has moved again."

Mollie tapped gently on the door, but received no response. Then she tried the knob, but the door was fastened.

"Nobody's home, I guess," she said.

"The back door is open," cried Whistlebinkie, running around to the rear of the house. "Come around this way, Mollie, and we can get in."

So around Mollie went, and sure enough there was the kitchen door standing wide open. A chicken was being grilled on the fire, and three eggs were in the pot boiling away so actively that they would undoubtedly have been broken had they not been boiling so long that they had become as hard as rocks.

"Isn't he the foolishest old man that ever was," said Mollie, as she caught sight of the chicken and the eggs. "That chicken will be burned to a crisp, and the eggs won't be fit to eat."

"I don't understand him at all," said Whistlebinkie. "Look at this notice to burglars he has pinned upon the wall."

Mollie looked and saw the following, printed in very awkward letters, hanging where Whistlebinkie had indicated:

NOTISS TO BURGYLERS.

If you have come to robb mi house you'd better save yourselfs the trouble. My silver spoons are all made of led, and my diamonds are only window glass. If you must steel something steel the boyled eggs, because I don't like boyled eggs anyhow. Also plese if you get overcome with remoss

for having robbed a poor old man like me
and want to give yourselfs upp to the poleese, you can ring up the poleese over the
tellyfone in Miss Mollie Wisslebinkie's
house up on Broadway.

Yoors trooly,

THE UNWISEMAN.

P. S. If you here me coming while you
are robbing me plese run, because I'm afraid
of burgylers, and doo not want to mete
enny.

N. G. If you can't rede my handwriting
you'd better get someboddy who can to tell
you what I have ritten, because it is very
important. Wishing you a plesant time I
am egen as I sed befour

Yoors tooly,

THE UNWISEMAN.

"What nonsense," said Mollie, as she
read this extraordinary production. "As if

52

the burglars would pay any attention to a notice like that."

"Oh, they might!" said Whistlebinkie. "It might make 'em laugh so they'd have fits, and then they couldn't burgle.

"It might make 'em laugh so they'd have fits; and then they couldn't burgle."

But what is that other placard he has pinned on the wall?"

"That," said Mollie, as she investigated

53

the second placard, "that seems to be a lot of rules for the kitchen. He's a queer old man for placards, isn't he?"

"Indeed he is," said Whistlebinkie. "What do the rules say?"

"I'll get 'em down," said Mollie, mounting a chair and removing the second placard from the wall. Then she and Whistlebinkie read the following words:

KITCHING RULES.

1. No cook under two years of age unaccompanied by nurse or parent aloud in this kitching.

3. Boyled eggs must never be cooked in the frying pan, and when fried eggs are ordered the cook must remember not to scramble them. This rule is printed ahed of number too, because it is more important than it.

2. Butcher boys are warned not to sit on the ranje while the fiyer is going because all

the heat in the fiyer is needed for cooking. Butcher boys who violate this rule will be charged for the cole con- sumed in burning them.

7. The fiyer must not be aloud to go out without some- boddy with it, be- cause fiyers are dangerous and might set

the house on fiyer. Any cook which lets the house burn down through voilating this rule will have the value of

"The fiyer must not be allowed to go out with- out someboddy with it." the house subtracted from her next month's wages, with in-

55

terest at forety persent from the date of the flyer.

11. Brekfist must be reddy at all hours, and shall consist of boyled eggs or something else.

4. Wages will be pade according to work done on the following skale:

For cooking one egg one hour . . . . . 1 cent.
    "   "   " leg of lamb one week . 3 "
    "   " pann cakes per duzzen . . 2 "
    "   " gravey, per kwart . . . . . 1 "
  " stooing proons per hundred . . . . 2 "

In making up bills against me cooks must add the figewers right, and substract from the whole the following charges:

For rent of kitchchen per day . . . . 10 cents.
For use of pans and kittles . . . . . 15 "
For cole, per nugget . . . . 3 "
Matches, kindeling and gas per day . . 20 "
Food consoomed in tasting . . . . . 30 "
Sundries . . . . 50 "

13. These rules must be obayed.

Yoors Trooly,

THE UNWISEMAN.

P. S. Ennyboddy violating these rules will be scolded. Yoors Tooly,

THE UNWISEMAN.

Whistlebinkie was rolling on the floor convulsed with laughter by the time Mollie finished reading these rules. He knew enough about housekeeping to know how delightful they were, and if the Unwiseman could have seen him he would doubtless have been very much pleased at his appreciation.

"The funny part of it all is, though," said Mollie, "that the poor old man doesn't keep a cook at all, but does all his own housework."

"Let's see what kind of a dining-room he has got," said Whistlebinkie, recovering from his convulsion. "I wonder which way it is."

"It must be in there to the right," said Mollie. "That is, it must if that sign in the passage-way means anything. Don't you see, Whistlebinkie, it says: 'This way to the dining-room,' and under it it has 'Caution: meals must not be served in the parlor'?"

"So it has," said Whistlebinkie, reading the sign. Let's go in there."

So the two little strangers walked into the dining-room, and certainly if the kitchen was droll in the matter of placards, the dining-room was more so, for directly over the table and suspended from the chandelier were these

RULES FOR GUESTS.

Guests will please remember to remove their hats before sitting down at the tabel.

Soup will not be helped more than three times to any guest, no matter who.

It is forbidding for guests to criticize the cooking, or to converse with the waiteress.

Guests will kindly not contradict or make fun of their host, since he is very irritable and does not like to be contradicted or made fun of. Guests will oblige their host by not asking for anything that is not on the bill of fare. In a

"Guest's will kindly not make fun of the host."

private house like this it would be very awkward to have to serve guests with fried potatoes at a time when ice-cream or mince pie has been ordered.

Horses and wheelbarrows are not aloud

in this diningroom under any circumstances whatever.

Neither must cows or hay scales be brought here. Guests bringing their own olives will be charged extra. Also their own assalted ammonds. Spoons, platters, and gravy boats taken from the table must be paid for at market rates for articles so taken away.

Any guest caught violating any or all of these rules will not be aloud any dessert whatever; and a second voilition will deprive them of a forth helping to roast beef and raisins.

Yoors Tooly,

THE UNWISEMAN.

N. G. Any guest desiring to substitute his own rules for the above is at libbity to do so, provided he furnishes his own diningroom.

"They're the most ridiculous rules I ever

heard of," said Mollie, with a grin so broad that it made her ears uncomfortable. "The idea of having to tell anybody not to wear a hat at the table! He might just as well have made a rule forbidding people to throw plates on the floor."

"I dessay he would have, if he'd thought of it," returned Whistlebinkie. "But just look at these rules for the waitress. They are worse than the others." Then Whistlebinkie read off the rules the Unwiseman had made for the waitress, as follows:

RULES FOR THE WAITERESS.

1. Iced water must never be served boiling, nor under any circumstances must ice-cream come to the tabel fried to a crisp.

2. Waiteresses caught upsetting the roast beef on a guest's lap will be charged for the beef at the rate of $1.00 a pound, and will have to go to bed without her brekfist.

3. All cakes, except lady-fingers, must be

61

served in the cake basket. The lady-fingers must be served in finger bowls, whether this is what the waiteress is used to or not. This is my dining-room, and I am the one to make the rules for it.

4. All waiteresses must wear caps. Their caps must be lace caps, and not yotting caps, tennis caps, or gun caps. The caps must be worn on the head, and not on the hands or feet. All waiteresses caught voilating this rule will not be allowed any pie for eight weeks.

5. Meals must not be served until they are ready, and such silly jokes as putting an empty soup tureen on the table for the purpose of fooling me will be looked upon with disfavor and not laughed at.

6. Waiteresses must never invite their friends here to take dinner with me unless I am out, and they mustn't do it then either, because this is my dining-room, and I can wear it out quick enough without any outside help.

7. Waiteresses must not whistle while waitering on the tabel, because it isn't proper that they should. Besides, girls can't whistle, anyhow.

8. At all meals dessert must be served at every other course. In serving a dinner this course should be followed:

    1. Pie.
    2. Soup.
    3. Custard.
    4. Roast Beef.
    5. Ice-cream.
    6. Sallad.
    7. Pudding.
    8. Coffee.
    9. More Pudding.

9. In case there is not enough of anything to go around more will be sent for at the waiteresses' expense, because the chances are she has been tasting it, which she hadn't any business to do.

10. To discourage waiteresses in losing spoons, and knives, and forks, any waiteress caught losing a spoon or a knife and a fork will have the price of two spoons, two knives, and two forks substracted off of her next month's wages.

Yoors Tooly,

THE UNWISEMAN.

N. G. All waiteresses who don't like these rules would better apply for some other place somewhere else, because I'm not going to take the trouble to get up a lot of good rules like these and then not have them obeyed. Riteing rules isn't easy work.

"Well I declare!" said Mollie, when they had finished reading. "I don't wonder he has to live in his little old house all by himself. I don't believe he'd get anybody to stay here a minute, if those rules had to be minded."

"Oh, I don't know," said Whistlebinkie. "They all seem reasonable enough."

"I think I'll take 'em down and show them to my mamma," said Mollie, reaching out to do as she said.

"No, no, don't do that," said Whistlebinkie. "T h a t wouldn't be right. They are his p r o p e r t y, and it would never do for you to steal them."

"Riteing rules isn't easy work."

"That's so," said Mollie. "I guess you are right."

"If you want to steal something why don't you do as he asked you to?" put in Whistlebinkie.

"What did he ask me to do?"

"Why don't you remember the notice to burglars?"

"Oh, yes!" said Mollie. "'If you must steal something steal a boyled egg.'"

"That's it. He doesn't like boyled eggs."

"And neither do I," said Mollie. "Particularly when they are as hard as bullets."

And then hearing the tinkle of the tea bell at home Mollie and Whistlebinkie left the Unwiseman's house without stealing anything, which after all was the best thing to do.

"Oh, yes!" said Mollie, "if you must steal something, steal a boyled egg."

—Page 66.

A CALL FROM THE UNWISEMAN *In which Mollie's call is returned.*

MOLLIE had been very busy setting things to rights in Cinderella's house one autumn afternoon not long after her visit to the Unwiseman. Cinderella was a careless Princess, who allowed her palace to get into a very untidy condition every two or three weeks. Bric-a-brac would be strewn here and there about the floor; clocks would be found standing upside down in the fire-places; andirons and shoe buttons would litter up the halls and obstruct the stairways

—in short, all things would get topsy-turvy within the doors of the Princess' house, and all because Princesses are never taught house-keeping. Should any King or Queen read these lines, the author hopes that his or her Majesty will take the hint and see to it that his or her daughters are

"Should any queen read these lines, the author hopes she will see that her daughter is brought up to look after household affairs."

properly brought up and taught to look after household affairs, for if they do not, most assuredly the time may come when the most magnificent palace in the world will be allowed to go to ruin through mere lack of attention.

It was a long and hard task for the little mistress of the nursery, but she finally accomplished it; apple-pie order once more ruled in the palace, the Princess' diamonds had been swept up from the floor, and stored away in the bureau drawers, and Mollie was taking a well-earned rest in her rocking-chair over by the window. As she gazed out upon the highway upon which the window fronted, she saw in the dim light a strange shadow passing down the walk, and in a minute the front door-bell rang. Supposing it to be no one but the boy with the evening paper, Mollie did not stir as she would have done if it had been her papa returning home. The paper boy possessed very little interest to her—indeed, I may go so far as to say that Mollie despised the paper boy, not because he was a paper boy, but because he was rude, and had, upon several occasions recently made faces at her and told her she didn't know anything because she was a girl, and other mean things like that; as if being a girl kept one from finding out useful and important things. So, as I have said, she sat still and gazed thoughtfully out of the window.

Her thoughts were interrupted in a moment, however, by a most extraordinary proceeding at the nursery door. It suddenly flew open with a bang, and Whistlebinkie came tumbling in head over heels, holding the silver card-receiver in his hand, and whistling like mad from excitement.

"Cardfew," he tooted through the top of his hat. "Nwiseman downstairs."

"What are you trying to say, Whistlebinkie?" asked Mollie, severely.

"Here is a card for you," said Whistlebinkie, standing up and holding out the salver upon which lay, as he had hinted, a card. "The gentleman is below."

Mollie picked up the card, which read this way :

| Mr. ME. | |
| | My House. |

"What on earth does it mean?" cried Mollie, with a smile, the card seemed so droll.

"It is the Unwiseman's card. He has called on you, and is downstairs in the parlor—and dear me, how funny he does look," roared Whistlebinkie breathlessly. "He's got on a beaver hat, a black evening coat like your papa wears to the theatre or to dinners, a pair of goloshes, and white tennis trousers. Besides that he's got an umbrella with him, and he's sitting in the parlor with it up over his head."

Whistlebinkie threw himself down on the floor in a spasm of laughter as he thought of the Unwiseman's appearance. Mollie meanwhile was studying the visitor's card.

71

"What does he mean by 'My House'?" she asked.

"That's his address, I suppose," said Whistlebinkie. "But what shall I tell him? Are you in?"

"Of course I'm in," Mollie replied, and before Whistlebinkie could get upon his feet again she had flown out of the room, down the stairs to the parlor, where, sure enough, as Whistlebinkie had said, the Unwiseman sat, his umbrella raised above his head, looking too prim and absurd for anything.

"How do you do, Miss Whistlebinkie?" he said, gravely, as Mollie entered the room. "I believe that is the correct thing to say when you are calling, though for my part I can't see why. People do so many things that there's a different way to do almost all of them. If I said, 'how do you do your sums?' of course there could be a definite answer. 'I do them by adding, or by substracting.' If any one calling on me should

72

say, 'how do you do?' I'd say, 'excuse me, but how do I do what?' However, I wish to be ruled by etiquette, and as I understand that is the proper question to begin with, I will say again, 'how do you do, Miss Whistlebinkie?' According to my etiquette book it is your turn to reply, and what you ought to say is, 'I'm very well, I thank you, how are you?' I'm very well."

"I'm delighted to hear it, Mr. Me," returned Mollie, glad of the chance to say something. "I have thought a great deal about you lately."

"So have I," said the Unwiseman. "I've been thinking about myself all day. I like to think about pleasant things. I've been intending to return your call for a long time, but really I didn't know exactly how to do it. You see, some things are harder to return than other things. If I borrowed a book from you, and wanted to return it, I'd know how in a minute. I'd just take the

73

book, wrap it up in a piece of brown paper, and send it back by mail or messenger—or both, in case it happened to be a male messenger. Same way with a pair of and-irons. Just return 'em by sending 'em back —but calls are different, and that's what I've come to see you about. I don't know how to return that call."

"But this is the return of the call," said Mollie.

"I don't see how," said the Unwiseman, with a puzzled look on his face. "This isn't the same call at all. The call you made at my house was another one. This arrange-ment is about the same as it would be in the case of my borrowing a book on Asparagus from you, and returning a book on Sweet Potatoes to you. That wouldn't be a return of your book. It would be returning *my* book. Don't you see? Now, I want to be polite and return your call, but I can't. I can't find it. It's come and gone. I almost

74

wish you hadn't called, it's puzzled me so. Finally, I made up my mind to come here, and apologize to you for not returning it. That's all I can do."

"Don't mention it," said Mollie.

"Oh, but I must! How could I apologize without mentioning it?" said the Unwiseman, hastily. "You wouldn't know what I was apologizing for if I didn't mention it. How have you been?"

"Quite well," said Mollie. "I've been very busy this fall getting my dolls' dresses made and setting everything to rights. Won't you—ah—won't you put down your umbrella, Mr. Me?"

"No, thank you," said the Unwiseman, with an anxious peep at the ceiling. "I am very timid about other people's houses, Miss Whistlebinkie. I have been told that sometimes houses fall down without any provocation, and while I don't doubt that your house is well built and all that, some nail somewhere might give way and the whole thing might come down. As long as I have the umbrella over my head I am safe, but without it the ceiling, in case the house did fall, would be likely to spoil my hat. This is a pretty parlor you have. They call it white and gold, I believe."

"Yes," said Mollie. "Mamma is very fond of parlors of that kind."

"So am I," said the Unwiseman. "I have one in my own house."

"Indeed?" said Mollie. "I didn't see it."

"You were in it, only you didn't know it," observed the Unwiseman. "It was that room with the walls painted brown. I was afraid the white and gold walls would get spotted if I didn't do something to protect them, so I had a coat of brown paint put over the whole room. Good idea that, I think, and all mine, too. I'd get it patented, if I wasn't afraid somebody would make an improvement on it, and get all the money

"No, thank you," said the unwiseman, with an anxious peep at the ceiling.—Page 76.

that belonged to me, which would make me very angry. I don't like to get angry, because when I do I always break something valuable, and I find that when I break any-thing valuable I get angrier than ever, and go ahead and break something else. If I got angry once I never could stop until I'd broken all the valuable things in the world, and when they were all gone where would I be?"

"I don't like to get angry."

"But it seems to me," said Mollie, as she puzzled over the Unwiseman's idea, of which he seemed unduly proud, "it seems to me that if you cover a white and gold parlor with a coat of brown paint, it doesn't stay a white and gold parlor. It becomes a brown parlor."

77

"Not at all," returned the Unwiseman. "How do you make that out? Put it this way: You, for instance, are a white girl, aren't you?"

"Yes," said Mollie.

"That is, they call you white, though really you are a pink girl. However, for the sake of the argument, you are white."

"Certainly," said Mollie, anxious to be instructed.

"And you wear clothes to protect you."

"I do."

"Now if you wore a brown dress, would you cease to be a white girl and become a nigrio?"

"A what?" cried Mollie.

"A nigrio—a little brown darky girl," said the Unwiseman.

"No," said Mollie. "I'd still be a white or pink girl, whatever color I was before."

"Well—that's the way with my white and gold parlor. It's white and gold, and I give

78

it a brown dress for protection. That's all there is to it. I see you keep your vases on the mantel-piece. Queer notion that. Rather dangerous, I should think."

Mollie laughed.

"Dangerous?" she cried. "Why not at all. They're safe enough, and the mantel-piece is the place for them, isn't it? Where do you keep yours?"

"I don't have any. I don't believe in 'em," replied the Unwiseman. "They aren't any good."

"They're splendid," said Mollie. "They're just the things to keep flowers in."

"What nonsense," said the Unwiseman, with a sneer. "The place to keep flowers is in a garden. You might just as well have a glass trunk in your parlor to hold your clothes in; or a big china bin to hold oats or grass in. It's queer how you people who know things do things. But anyhow, if I did have vases I wouldn't put 'em on man-

79

tel-pieces, but on the floor. If they are on
the floor they can't fall off and break unless
your house turns
upside down."

"They might
get stepped on,"
said Mollie.

"Poh!" snapped
the Unwiseman.
"Don't you
wise people
look where
you step?
I do, and
they say I
don't know
enough to
go in when
it rains,
which is not
true. I know more than enough to go in
when it rains. I stay out when it rains be-

"I'm fond of the wet."

cause I like to. I'm fond of the wet. It keeps me from drying up, and makes my clothes fit me. Why, if I hadn't stayed out in the rain every time I had a chance last summer my flannel suit never would have fitted me. It was eight sizes too big, and it took sixteen drenching storms to make it shrink small enough to be just right. Most men—wise men they call themselves—would have spent money having them misfitted again by a tailor, but I don't spend my money on things I can get done for nothing. That's the reason I don't pay anything out to beggars. I can get all the begging I want done on my place without having to pay a cent for it, and yet I know lots and lots of people who are all the time spending money on beggars."

"There is a great deal in what you say," said Mollie.

"There generally is," returned the Unwiseman. "I do a great deal of thinking, and I don't say anything without having thought it all out beforehand. That's why I'm so glad you were at home to-day. I mapped out all my conversation before I came. In fact, I wrote it all down, and then learned it by heart. It would have been very unpleasant if after doing all that, taking all that trouble, I should have found you out. It's very disappointing to learn a conversation, and then not converse it."

"I should think so," said Mollie. "What do you do on such occasions? Keep it until the next call?"

"No. Sometimes I tell it to the maid, and ask her to tell it to the person who is out. Sometimes I say it to the front door, and let the person it was intended for find it out for herself as best she can, but most generally I send it to 'em by mail."

Here the Unwiseman paused for a minute, cocking his head on one side as if to think.

"Excuse me," he said. "But I've for-gotten what I was to say next. I'll have to consult my memorandum-book. Hold my umbrella a minute—over my head please. Thank you."

Then as Mollie did as the queer creature wished, he fumbled in his pockets for a minute and shortly extracting his memoran-dum-book from a mass of other stuff, he consulted its pages.

"Oh, yes!" he said, with a smile of happi-ness. "Yes, I've got it now. At this point you were to ask me if I wouldn't like a glass of lemonade, and I was to say yes, and then you were to invite me up-stairs to see your play room. There's some talk scattered in during the lemonade, but, of course, I can't go on until you've done your part."

He gazed anxiously at Mollie for a mo-ment, and the little maid, taking the hint, smilingly said:

"Ah! won't you have a little refreshment,

83

Mr. Me? A glass of lemonade, for in-stance?"

"Why—ah—certainly, Miss Whistlebin-kie. Since you press me, I—ah—I don't care if I do."

And the caller and his hostess passed, laughing heartily, out of the white and gold parlor into the pantry.

THE UNWISEMAN IS OFFENDED

In which the Old Gentleman takes his leave

"How do you like your lemonade?" asked Mollie, as she and the Unwiseman entered the pantry. "Very sour or very sweet?"

"What did you invite me to have?" the Unwiseman replied. "Lemonade or sugarade?"

"Lemonade, of course," said Mollie. "I never heard of sugarade before."

"Well, lemonade should be very lemony and sugarade should be very sugary; so when I am invited to have lemonade I naturally expect something very lemony, don't I?"

"I suppose so," said Mollie, meekly.

"Very well, then. That answers your question. I want it very sour. So sour that I can't drink it without it puckering my mouth up until I can't do anything but whistle like our elastic friend with the tootle in his hat."

"You mean Whistlebinkie?" said Mollie.

"Yes—that India-rubber creature who follows you around all the time and squeaks whenever any one pokes him in the ribs. What's become of him? Has he blown himself to pieces, or has he gone off to have himself made over into a golosh?"

"Oh, no—Whistlebinkie is still here," said Mollie. "In fact, he let you into the house. Didn't you see him?"

"No, indeed I didn't," said the Unwiseman. "What do you take me for? I'm proud, I am. I wouldn't look at a person who'd open a front door. I come of good family. My father was a Dunderberg and my mother was a Van Scootle. We're one of the oldest families in creation. One of my ancestors was in the Ark, and I had several who were not. It would never do for one in my position to condescend to see a person who opened a front door for pay.

"That's why I don't have servants in my own house. I'd have to speak to them, and the idea of a Dunderberg-Van Scootle engaged in any kind of conversation with servants is not to be thought of. We never did anything for pay in all the history of our family, and we never recognize as equals people who do. That's why I have nothing to do with anybody but children. Most grown up people work."

"I don't see how you live," said Mollie. "How do you pay your bills?"

"Don't have any," said the Unwiseman.

"Never had a bill in my life. I leave bills to canary birds and mosquitoes."

"But you have to buy things to eat, don't you?"

"Very seldom," said the Unwiseman. I'm never hungry; but when I do get hungry I can most generally find something to eat somewhere—apples, for instance. I can live a week on one apple."

"Well, what do you do when you've eaten the apple?" queried Mollie.

"What an absurd question," laughed the Unwiseman. "Didn't you know that there was more than one apple in the world? Every year I find enough apples to last me as long as I think it is necessary to provide. Last year I laid in fifty-three apples so that if I got very hungry one week I could have two—or maybe I could give a dinner and invite my friends, and they could have the extra apple. Don't you see?"

"Well, you are queer, for a fact!" said

Mollie, getting a large lemon out of the pantry closet and cutting it in half.

As the sharp steel blade of the knife cut through the crisp yellow lemon the eyes of the Unwiseman opened wide and bulged with astonishment.

"What on earth are you doing, Miss Whistlebinkie?" he said. "Why do you destroy that beautiful thing?"

It was Mollie's turn to be surprised.

"I don't know what you mean" she said. "Why shouldn't I cut the lemon? How can I make a lemonade without cutting it?"

"Humph!" said the Unwiseman, with a half sneer on his lips. "You'll go to the poor-house if you waste things like that. Why, I've had lemonade for a year out of one lemon, and it hasn't been cut open yet. I drop it in a glass of water and let it soak for ten minutes. That doesn't use up the lemon juice as your plan does, and it makes one of the bitterest sour drinks that you ever

89

drank—however, this is your lemonade treat, and it isn't for me to criticize. My book of etiquette says that people out calling must act according to the rules of the house they are calling at. If you asked me to have some oyster soup and then made it out of sassafras or snow-balls, it would be my place to eat it and say I never tasted better oyster soup in my life. That's a funny thing about being polite. You have to do and say so many things that you don't really mean. But go ahead. Make your lemonade in your own way. I've got to like it whether I like it or not. It isn't my lemon you are wasting."

Mollie resumed the making of the lemonade while the Unwiseman looked about him, discovering something that was new and queer to him every moment. He seemed to be particularly interested in the water pipes.

"Strange idea that," he said, turning the cold water on and off all the time. "You have a little brook running through your house whenever you want it. Ever get any fish out of it?"

"No," said Mollie, with a laugh. "We couldn't get very big fish through a faucet that size."

"That's what I was thinking," said the Unwiseman, turning the water on again; "and furthermore, I think it's very strange that you don't fix it so that you can get fish.

A trout "Why don't you have larger faucets and catch the fish?"

isn't more than four inches around. You could get one through a six-inch pipe with-

91

out any trouble unless he got mad and stuck his fins out. Why don't you have larger faucets and catch the fish? I would. If there aren't any fish in the brook you can stock it up without any trouble, and it would save you the money you pay to fish-markets as well as the nuisance of going fishing yourself and putting worms on hooks."

A long hilarious whistle from the pantry door caused the Unwiseman to look up sharply.

"What was that?" he said.

"Smee," came the whistling voice.

"It's Whistlebinkie," said Mollie.

"Is his real name Smee?" asked the Unwiseman. "I thought Whistlebinkie was his name."

"So it is," said Mollie. "But when he gets excited he always runs his words together and speaks them through the top of his hat. By 'smee' he meant 'it's me.' Come in, Whistlebinkie."

"I shall not notice him," said the Unwiseman, stiffly. "Remember what I said to you about my family. He opens front doors for pay."

"Donteither," whistled Whistlebinkie.

"You wrong him, Mr. Unwiseman," said Mollie. "He isn't paid for opening the front door. He just does it for fun."

"Oh! well, that's different," said the proud visitor. "If he does it just for fun I can afford to recognize him—though I must say I can't see what fun there is in opening front doors. How do you do, Whistlebinkie?"

"Pretwell," said Whistlebinkie. "How are you?"

"I hardly know what to say," replied the Unwiseman, scratching his head thoughtfully. "You see, Miss Mollie, when I got up my conversation for this call I didn't calculate on Whistlebinkie here. I haven't any remarks prepared for him. Of course, I could tell him that I am in excellent health, and that I think possibly it will rain before the year is over; but, after all, that's very ordinary kind of talk, and we'll have to keep changing the subject all the time to get back to my original conversation with you."

"Whistlebinkie needn't talk at all," said Mollie. "He can just whistle."

"Or maybe I could go outside and put in a few remarks for him here and there, and begin the call all over again," suggested the Unwiseman.

"Oh, no! Dodoothat," began Whistlebinkie.

"Now what does he mean by dodoothat?" asked the visitor, with a puzzled look on his face.

"He means don't do that—don't you, Whistlebinkie? Answer plainly through your mouth and let your hat rest," said Mollie.

"That—swat—I—meant," said Whistlebinkie, as plainly as he could. "He—needn't —botherto—talk—toomee—to me, I mean. I only—want—to—listen—towhim."

"What's towhim?" asked the Unwiseman.

"To you is what he means. He says he's satisfied to listen to you when you talk."

"Thassit," Whistlebinkie hurried to say, meaning, I suppose, "that's it."

"Ah!" said the Unwiseman, with a pleased smile. "That's it, eh? Well, permit me to say that I think you are a very wonderfully wise rubber doll, Mr. Whistlebinkie. I may go so far as to say that in this view of the case I think you are the wisest rubber doll I ever met. You like my conversation, do you?"

"Deedido," whistled Whistlebinkie. "I think it's fine!"

"I owe you an apology, Whistlebinkie," said the Unwiseman, gazing at the doll in an affectionate way. "I thought you opened front doors for pay, instead of which I find that you are one of the wisest, most interesting rubber celebrities of the day. I apologize for even thinking that you would accept pay for opening a front door, and I will esteem it a great favor if you will let me be your friend. Nay, more. I shall make it my first task to get up a conversation especially for you. Eh? Isn't that fine, Whistlebinkie? I, Me, the Unwiseman, promise to devote fifteen or twenty minutes of his time to getting up talk for you, talk with thinking in it, talk that amounts to something, talk that ninety-nine talkers out of a hundred conversationalists couldn't say if they tried; and all for you. Isn't that honor?"

"Welliguess!" whistled Whistlebinkie.

"Very well, then. Listen," said the Unwiseman. "Where were we at, Miss Mollie?"

"I believe," said Mollie, squeezing a half a lemon, "I believe you were saying something about putting fish through the faucet."

"Oh, yes! As I remember it, the faucets were too small to get the fish through, and I was wondering why you didn't have them larger."

"That was it," said Mollie. "You thought if the faucets were larger it would save fish-hooks and worms."

"Exactly," said the Unwiseman. "And I wonder at it yet. I'd even go farther. If I could have a trout-stream running through my house that I could turn on and off as I pleased, I'd have also an estuary connected with the Arctic regions through which whales could come, and in that way I'd save lots of money. Just think what would happen if you could turn on a faucet and get a whale. You'd get oil enough to supply every lamp in your house. You wouldn't have to pay gas bills or oil bills, and besides all that you could have whale steaks for breakfast, and whenever your mother wanted any whale-bone, instead of sending to the store for it, she'd have plenty in the house. If you only caught one whale a month, you'd have all you could possibly need."

"It certainly is a good idea," said Mollie. "But I don't think——"

"Wait a minute, please," said the Unwiseman, hastily. "That don't think remark of yours isn't due until I've turned on this other faucet."

Suiting his action to his word, the Unwiseman turned on the hot-water faucet, and plunging his hand into the water, slightly scalded his fingers.

"Ouch!" he cried. "The brook must be afire! Now who ever heard of that? The idea of a brook being on fire! Really, Miss Whistlebinkie, you ought to tell your papa about this. If you don't, the pipes will melt and who knows what will become of your house? It will be flooded with burning water!"

"Oh, no!—I guess not. That water is

"Ouch!" he cried; "the brook must be afire!"—Page 98.

heated down stairs in the kitchen, in the boiler."

"But—but isn't it dangerous?" the Unwiseman asked, anxiously.

"Not at all," said Mollie. "You've been mistaken all along, Mr. Me. There isn't any brook running through this house."

"I?" cried the Unwiseman, indignantly. "Me? I? The Unwiseman mistaken? Never! I never made a mistake but once, Miss Mary J. Whistlebinkie, and that was in calling upon you. I'm going home at once. You have outrageously offended me."

"I didn't mean to," pleaded Mollie. "I was only trying to tell you the truth. This water comes out of a tank."

"Excuse me," said the Unwiseman, indignantly. "You have said that I have made a mistake. You charge me with an act of which I have never been guilty, and I am going straight home. You said something

99

that wasn't in the conversation, and we can never get back again to the point from which you have departed."

"I am going straight home."

"Oh! do stay," said Whistlebinkie. "You haven't seen the nursery yet, and the hardwood stairs, and all the lovely things we have here."

"No, I haven't— and I sha'n't now!" retorted the Unwiseman. "I had some delicious remarks to make about the nursery, but now they are impossible. I shall not even drink your lemonade. I am going home!"

And without another word the Unwiseman departed in high dudgeon.

"Isn't it too bad," said Mollie, as she heard the front door slam after the departing guest.

"Yes," said Whistlebinkie. "I wanted him to stay until it was dark. I should like so much to know what he'd have to say about gas."

VI

THE CHRISTMAS VENTURE OF THE UNWISEMAN

In which the Unwiseman goes into an unprofitable business

It was the Saturday before Christmas. Mollie and Whistlebinkie started out in the afternoon to watch the boys skating for a while, after which they went to the top of the great hill just outside the village to take a coast or two. Whistle-binkie had never had any experience on a sled, and he was very anxious to try it just once, and, as Mollie was a little sleepy when he began persuading her to take him some time when she went, for the sake of peace and rest she had immediately promised what he wished of her. So here they were, on this cold, crisp December day, laboriously lugging Mollie's sled up the hill.

"Tain-teesy!" whistled Whistlebinkie.

"What's that you say?" panted Mollie, for she was very much out of breath.

"Tain-teesy," repeated Whistlebinkie. "I can't wissel well when I'm out of breath."

"Well, I guess I know what you mean," said Mollie. "You mean that it isn't easy pulling this sled up hill."

"Thassit!" said Whistlebinkie. "If this is what you call coasting, I don't want any more of it."

"Oh, no!" said Mollie. "This isn't coasting. This is only getting ready to coast. The coast comes when you slide down hill. We'll come down in about ten seconds."

"Humph!" said Whistlebinkie. "All this pulling and hauling for ten seconds' worth of fun?"

"That's what I say!" said a voice at Mollie's elbow. "Sliding down hill is never any fun unless you live at the top of the hill and wish to go down to the

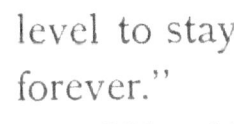

level to stay forever."

"Why," cried Mollie, delightedly, as she recognized the voice; "why it's the Unwiseman!"

"Sotiz!" roared Whistlebinkie, intending, of course, to say "so it is."

"Sliding down hill is never any fun unless you live at the top of the hill."

"Certainly it is," said the Unwiseman; "for how could it be otherwise, seeing as I am not a magic lantern and so cannot change myself into some one else? I've got to stay Me always."

105

"Magic lanterns can't change themselves into anything else," said Mollie. "You must mean magician."

"Maybe I must," said the Unwiseman. "I guess you are right. Some people call 'em by a long name like prestodigipotatoes, but your word is good enough for me, so we'll let it go at that. I'm not a magellan, so I can't transfigure myself. Therefore, I am still the Unwiseman at your service. But tell me, are you going sliding?"

"Yes," said Mollie. "Want to come with us?"

"I'd like to, but I'm afraid I can't. I'm very busy," replied the Unwiseman. "I'm going into business."

"You?" cried Mollie, in amazement. "Why, didn't you tell me once that you never worked? That no member of your family had ever worked, and that you despised trade?"

"Iyeardim," put in Whistlebinkie.

106

"What's that?" queried the Unwiseman, frowning at Whistlebinkie. "What does iyeardim mean?"

"It's Whistlebinkie for 'I heard him,'" explained Mollie. "He means to say that he heard you say you had never worked and never intended to."

"No doubt," said the Unwiseman. "No doubt. But misfortune has overtaken me. I have ceased to like apples."

"Ho!" laughed Mollie. "What has that to do with it?"

"I have ceased to like apples and have conceived an unquenchable thirst for chocolate eclaires," said the Unwiseman. "Hitherto, as I once told you, I have lived on apples, which cost me nothing, because I could pick them up in the orchard, but chocolate eclaires cost money. I have been informed, and I believe, they cost five cents a piece; that they do not grow on trees, but are made by men calling themselves fakirs——"

"Bakers, you mean, I guess," interrupted Mollie.

"It may be," said the Unwiseman, "though neither fakir nor baker seems to me to be so good a name for a man who makes cakes as the word caker."

"But there isn't any such word," said Mollie.

"Then that accounts for it," said the Unwiseman. "If there were such a word those men would be called by it. But to come back to the chocolate eclaires, whether they are made by bakers, fakirs, or plumbers, they cost money; if I don't have them I shall starve to death, for I can never more eat apples; therefore, to live I must make some money, and to make money I must go into business."

"Well, I haven't any doubt it will be good for you," said Mollie. "It's always well to have something to do. What business are you going into?"

"Ah!" said the Unwiseman, with a shake of his head. "That's my secret. I've got a patent business I'm going into. It's my own invention. I was going to be a lawyer at first, but I heard that lawyers gave advice. I don't intend to give anything. There isn't any money in giving things, so, of course, I decided not to be a lawyer—besides, I know of a man who was a lawyer and he spent all of his life up to his ears in trouble, and he didn't even own the trouble. It all belonged to his victims."

"Why don't you become a minister?" suggested Mollie.

"That's too hard work," said the Unwiseman. "You've got to go to church three times every Sunday, and, besides, my house wouldn't look well with a steeple on it. Then, too, I'd have to take a partner to ring the bell and play the organ, and, of course, he'd want half the collections. No: I couldn't be a minister. I'm too droll to be

one, even if my house would look well with
a steeple on it. I did think some of being a
doctor, though."

"Why don't you?" said Mollie. "Doctors
are awfully nice people. Our doctor is just
lovely. He gives me the nicest medicines
you ever saw."

"That may be true; but I don't want to be
a doctor," returned the Unwiseman. "You
have to study an awful lot to be a doctor. I
knew a man once who studied six weeks
before he could be a doctor, and then what
do you suppose happened? It was awfully
discouraging."

"What was it?" queried Mollie.

"Why, he practised on a cat he owned, to
see what kind of a doctor he had become,
and the cat died all nine times at once; so
the poor fellow, after wasting all those weeks
on study, had to become a plumber, after all.
Plumbing is the easiest profession of all, you
know. You don't have to know anything to

be a plumber, only you've got to have strong eyes."

" I didn't know that," said Mollie.

"Oh my, yes!" returned the Unwiseman. "You can't be a plumber unless you have strong eyes. It is very bad for a weak-eyed person to have to sit on the floor and look at a pipe all day. That is one reason why I'm not going to be a plumber. The other reason is that they never get any rest. They work all day eying pipes, and then have to sit up all night making out bills, and then they burn their fingers on stoves, and they sometimes get their feet wet after springing a leak on a pipe, and, altogether, it isn't pleasant. People play jokes on plumbers, too; mean jokes. Why, I knew a plumber who was called out in the middle of the night once by a city man who was trying to be a farmer during the summer months, and what do you suppose the trouble was?"

"I'm sure I don't know," said Mollie. "What?"

"The city man said he'd come home late and found the well full of water, and what was worse, the colander was riddled with holes. Twelve o'clock at night, mind you, and one of these bitter cold summer nights you find down in New Jersey."

"That was awfully mean," said Mollie. "That is, it was if the city man didn't know any better."

"He did know better. He did it just for a joke," said the Unwiseman.

"And didn t the plumber put in a great big bill for that?" asked Mollie.

"Yes—but the city man couldn't pay it," said the Unwiseman. "That was the meanest part of the joke. He went and lost all his money afterward. I believe he did it just to spite the plumber."

"Well," said Mollie, "here we are at the top of the hill at last. Won't you change your mind and go down with us, just once?"

"Nope," returned the Unwiseman. "I can't change my mind. Can't get it out of my head, to change. Besides, I must hurry. I've got to get a hundred pairs of stockings before Christmas Eve."

"Oh!" said Mollie. "I see. You are going into the stocking business."

"No, I'm not," said the queer old fellow, with a knowing smile. "There isn't much money in selling stockings. I've got a better idea than that. You come around to my house Christmas morning and I'll show you a thing or two—that is, I will if I can get the hundred pairs of stockings—you couldn't lend me a few pairs, could you?"

"I guess maybe so," said Mollie.

"All right—thank you very much," said the Unwiseman. "I'll be off now and get them. Good-by."

And before Mollie could say another word he was gone.

"Isn't he the worst you ever saw?" said Mollie.

"Puffickly-digulous," said Whistlebinkie.

"I wonder what his business is to be," observed Mollie, as she seated herself on the sled and made ready for the descent.

"I haven't the slightest ideeeee-eeeeeeee-eeeee-eeee-ah!" whistled Whistlebinkie; a strange and long-drawn-out word that; but whistling dolls are very like boys and girls when they are sliding down hill. Mollie had set the sled in motion just as Whistlebinkie started to speak, and her little rubber companion could not get away from the letter *e* in idea until he and his mistress ran plump into the snow-drift at the foot of the hill.

"My!" said Whistlebinkie, blowing the snow out of his whistle. "Wasn't that fine! I could do that all day."

"You could if the hill was long enough,"

said Mollie, sagely. " But come, we must go home now." And home they went.

In the forty-eight or more hours that passed before Christmas morning came, Mollie often wondered at the business venture of the Unwiseman. What it could be she could not guess. The hundred pairs of stockings mystified her exceedingly, and so, when Christmas morning finally dawned, the first thing she and Whistlebinkie did was to post off at full speed to the house of the Unwiseman.

" I wonder where his home is now ?" said Whistlebinkie, as they walked along.

" I haven't the slightest idea," said Mollie ; "but it's had a way of turning up where we least expected it in the past, so maybe we'll find it in the same way now."

Mollie was right, for hardly were the words out of her mouth when directly in front of her she saw what was unmistakably the house of the Unwiseman, only fastened to the chimney was a huge sign, which had not been there the last time she and Whistlebinkie had visited the Unwiseman.

"What is that he's got on his chimmilly?" said Whistlebinkie, who did not know how to spell, and who always pronounced words as he thought they were spelled.

"It's a sign—sure as you live," said Mollie.

"What does it say?" Whistlebinkie asked.

"The Unwiseman's Orphan Asylum," said Mollie, reading the sign. "Notice to Santa Claus: Dear Sir:—Too Hundred Orphans is Incarcerated Here. Please leave Toys Accordingly."

"Ho!" said Whistlebinkie. "How queer."

"You don't suppose he has really gone into the Orphan Asylum business?" said Mollie.

"I dono," said Whistlebinkie. "Let's wait till we see him before we decide."

So they ran on until they got to the Unwiseman's front door, upon which they knocked as hard as they knew how.

"Who's there?" came a reply in a mournful voice, from within.

"It's us," said Mollie.

"Who is Uss?" said the voice. "I know several Usses. Are you George W. Uss, the trolley-car conductor, or William Peters Uss, the poet? If you are the poet, I don't want to see you. I don't care for any poetry to-day. If you are the conductor, I've paid my fare."

"It's Mollie and Whistlebinkie," said Mollie.

"Oh—well, that's different. Come in and see your poor ruined old friend, who's got to go back to apples, whether he likes them or not," said the voice.

Mollie opened the door and walked in, Whistlebinkie following close behind her—and what a sight it was that met their gaze! There in the middle of the floor sat the

Unwiseman, the perfect picture of despair. Scattered about the room were hundreds of broken toys, and swinging from the mantel-piece were two hundred stockings.

"Hello!" said the Unwiseman. "Merry Christmas. I'm ruined; but what of that? You aren't."

"But how are you ruined?" asked Mollie.

"My business has failed—it didn't work," groaned the Unwiseman. "It was the toy business I was going into, and as I had no money to buy the toys with I borrowed a hundred pairs of stockings and hung 'em up. Then I put out that notice for Santa Claus, telling him that this was an Orphan Asylum."

"Yes," said Mollie, "I know. But it wasn't the truth, was it?"

"Of course it was," said the Unwiseman. "I'm an orphan. Very few men of my age are not, and this is my asylum."

"Yes; but you said there were two hundred in here," said Mollie. "I saw your sign."

"Well there are," said the Unwiseman. "The piano hasn't any father or mother, neither have the chairs, or the hundred and ninety-

The Unwiseman's "orphans."

eight other orphans in this house. It was all true."

"Well, anyhow," said Whistlebinkie, "you've got heaps of things. Every stocking seems to have been filled."

"True," said the Unwiseman. "But almost entirely with old, cast-off toys. I think it's pretty mean that boys and girls who are not orphans should get all the new toys and that those who are orphans get the broken ones."

Which strikes me as a very wise remark for an unwise man to make.

"Anyhow," continued the Unwiseman, "I'm ruined. I can't sell these toys, and so I've got to go back to apples."

And here he fell to weeping so violently that Mollie and Whistlebinkie stole softly out and went home; but on the way Mollie whispered to Whistlebinkie:

"I'm rather sorry for him; but, after all, it was his own fault. He really did try to deceive Santa Claus."

"Yes," said Whistlebinkie. "That's so. But he was right about the meanness of giving only old toys to orphans."

"Yes, he was," said Mollie.

"Yesindeedy!" whistled Whistlebinkie through his hat, gleefully, for he was very happy, as indeed I should be, if I were an old toy, to hear my little master or mistress say it was mean to give me away.

"By the way," said Mollie. "He seems to have got over his anger with us. I was afraid he wouldn't ever speak to us again after his call."

"So was I," said Whistlebinkie. "And I asked him if he wasn't mad at us any more, and he said, yes he was, but he'd forgiven us for our Christmas present."

VII

The Unwiseman's New Year's Resolutions

In which the Unwiseman gives up some very distinguished words.

DURING the days immediately following Christmas Mollie was so absorbed in the beautiful things the season of peace on earth and good will to men had brought to her that she not only forgot the Unwiseman and his woe over the failure of his business plans, but even her poor little friend Whistlebinkie was allowed to lie undisturbed and unthought of. Several times when she had come near his side Whistlebinkie had tried to whistle something in her ear, but unsuc-

123

cessfully. Either the something he wanted to whistle wouldn't come, or else if it did Mollie failed to hear it, and Whistlebinkie was very unhappy in consequence.

"That's always the way," he sobbed to Flaxilocks who shared his exile with him and who sat on the toy shelf gazing jealously out of her great, deep blue eyes at the magnificent new wax doll that Mollie had received from her grandmother; "don't make any difference how fine a toy may be, he may be made of the best of rubber, and have a whistle that isn't equalled by any locomotive whistle in the world for sweetness, the time comes when his master or mistress grows tired of him and lavishes all her affection on another toy because the other toy happens to be new. What on earth she can see in that real dog to admire I cannot discern. He can't bark half so well as I can whistle, and I am in mortal terror of him all the time, he eyes me so hungrily—but now he is her favorite. Everywhere Mollie goes Gyp goes, and I'm real mad."

"Oh, never mind," said Flaxilocks; "she'll get tired of him in a week or two and then she'll take us up again, just as if we were new. I've been around other Christmases and I know how things work. It'll be all right in a little while—that is, it will be for you. I don't know how it is going to turn out with me. That new doll, while I can see many defects in her, which you can't, I can't deny is a beauty, and her earrings are much handsomer than mine. It may be that I must become second to her; but you, you needn't play second fiddle to any one, for there isn't another rubber doll with a whistle in his hat in the house to rival you."

"Well, I wish I could be sure of that," said Whistlebinkie, mournfully, "I can see very well how Mollie can love you as well as she loves me—but that real dog, bah! He can't even whistle, and he's awfully destructive. Only last night he chewed up the calico cat, and actually, Mollie laughed. Do you suppose she would laugh if he chewed me up?"

"He couldn't chew you up," said Flaxilocks. "You are rubber." Whistlebinkie was about to reply to this when his fears were set at rest and Flaxilocks was comforted, for Mollie with her new dog and wax doll came up to where they were sitting and introduced her new pets to the old ones.

"I want you four to know each other," she said. "We'll have lots of fun together this year," and then before they knew it Flaxilocks and the new doll were fast friends, and as for Whistlebinkie and Gyp, they became almost inseparable. Gyp barked and Whistlebinkie whistled, while the dolls sat holding each other's hands, looking if anything quite as happy as Mollie herself.

"What do you all say to making a call on

the Unwiseman?" Mollie said, after a few minutes. "We ought to go wish him a Happy New Year."

"Simply elegant," whistled Whistlebinkie, and Gyp and the dolls said he was right, and so they all started off together.

So they all started off together.

"Where does he live?" asked the new doll.

"All around," said Flaxilocks. "He has a house that moves about. One day it is in one place and another in another."

"But how do you find it?" queried the new doll.

127

"You don't have to," whistled Whistle-binkie. "You just walk on until you run against it,"—and just as he spoke, as if to prove his words, bang! he ran right into the gate. "Here it is now," he added.

"He evidently doesn't want to see any-body," said Mollie, noticing a basket hanging from the front door-knob. "He's put out a basket for cards. Dear me! I wish he'd see us."

"Maybe he will," said Whistlebinkie. "I'll ring the bell. Hello!" he added sharply, as he looked into the basket; "that's queer. It's chock-up full of cards now—somebody must have called."

"It has a placard over it," said Flaxilocks.

"So it has," said Mollie, a broad smile brightening her face; "and it says, 'Take one' on it. What *does* he mean?"

"That looks like your card on top," said Flaxilocks.

"Why it *is* my card," cried Mollie, "and

here is Whistlebinkie's card too. We haven't been here."

"Of course you haven't," said a voice from behind the door. "But you are here now. I knew you were coming and I was afraid you'd forget to bring your cards with you, so I took some of your old ones that you had left here before and put 'em out there where you could get them. Ring the bell, and I'll let you in."

Whistlebinkie rang the bell as instructed, and the door was immediately opened, and there stood the Unwiseman waiting to welcome them.

"Why, dear me! What a delicious surprise," he said. "Walk right in. I had no idea you were coming."

"We came to wish you a Happy New Year," said Mollie.

"That's very kind of you," said the Unwiseman, "very kind, indeed. I was thinking of you this morning when I was making

my good resolutions for the New Year. I
was wondering whether I ought to give you
up with other good things, and I finally
decided not to. One must have some com-
fort."

"Then you have made some good resolutions, have you?" said Mollie.

"Millions of 'em," said the Unwiseman;
"and I'm going to make millions more. One
of 'em is that I won't catch cold during the
coming year. That's one of the best resolutions a man of my age can make. Colds are
very bad things, and it costs so much to be
rid of them. Why, I had one last winter
and I had to burn three cords of wood to get
rid of it."

"Do you cure a cold with wood?" asked
Flaxilocks.

"Why not?" returned the Unwiseman.
"A roaring hot fire is the best cure for cold
I know. What do you do when you have a
cold, sit on the ice-box?"

"No, I take medicine," said Mollie. "Pills and things."

"I don't like pills," said the Unwiseman. "They don't burn well. I bought some quinine pills to cure my cold three winters ago, and they just sizzled a minute when I lit them and went out." This pleased Gyp so much that he sprang upon the piano and wagged his tail on C sharp until Mollie made him stop.

"Another resolution I made," continued the Unwiseman, "was to open that piano. That's why it's open now. I've always kept it locked before, but now it is going to be open all the time. That'll give the music a chance to get out; and it's a good thing for pianos to get a little fresh air once in a while. It's the stale airs in that piano—airs like Way Down Upon the Suwanee River, and Annie McGinty, and tunes like that that have made me dislike it."

"Queerest man I ever saw!" whispered the new doll to Flaxilocks.

"But I didn't stop there," said the Unwiseman. "I made up my mind that I wouldn't grow any older this year. I'm going to stay seven hundred, just as I am now, always. Seven hundred is old enough for anybody, and I'm not going to be greedy about my years when I have enough. Let somebody else have the years, say I."

"Very wise and very generous," said Mollie; "but I don't see just how you are going to manage it."

"Me neither," whistled Whistlebinkie. "I do'see how you're going to do that."

"Simple enough," said the Unwiseman. "I've stopped the clock."

Gyp turned his head to one side as the Unwiseman spoke and looked at him earnestly for a few seconds, and then, as if overcome with mirth at the idea, he rushed out of the door and chased his tail around the house three times.

"What an extraordinary animal that is," said the Unwiseman. "He must be very young."

"He is," said Mollie. "He is nothing but a puppy."

"Well, it seems to me he wastes a good deal of strength," said the Unwiseman. "Why, if I should run around the house that way three times I'd be so tired I'd have to hire a man to help me rest."

"Are you really seven hundred years old?" queried the new doll, who, I think, would have followed Gyp's example and run around the house herself if she had thought it was dignified and was not afraid of spoiling her new three-button shoes.

"I don't know for sure," said the Unwiseman, "but I fancy I must be. I know I'm over sixty because I was born seventy-three years ago. Seven hundred is over sixty, and so for the sake of round figures I have selected that age. It's rather a wonderful age, don't you think so ?"

"It certainly is," said the new doll.

"But then you are a wonderful man," said Mollie.

"True," said the Unwiseman, reflectively. "I am wonderful. Sometimes I spend the whole night full of wonder that I should be so wonderful. I know so much. Why, I can read French. I can't understand it, but I can read it quite as well as I can English. I can't read English very well, of course; but then I only went to school one day and that happened to be a holiday; so I didn't learn how to do anything but take a day off. But we are getting away from my resolutions. I want to tell you some more of them. I have thought it all over, and I am determined that all through the year I shall eat only three meals a day with five nibbles between times. I'm going to give up water-melons, which I never eat, and when I converse with anybody I have solemnly promised myself never to make use of such words as assafœdita, peristyle, or cosmopolis. That last resolution is a great sacrifice for me because I am very fond of long words. They sound so learned; but I shall be firm. Assafœdita, peristyle, and cosmopolis until next year dawns shall be dead to me. I may take them on again next year; but if I do, I shall drop Mulligatawney, Portuguese, and pollywog from my vocabulary. I may even go so far as to drop vocabulary, although it is a word for which I have a strong affection. I am so attached to vocabulary as a word that I find myself murmuring it to myself in the dead of night."

"What does it mean?" asked the new doll.

"Vocabulary?" cried the Unwiseman. "Vocabulary? Don't you know what a vocabulary is?"

"I know," said Whistlebinkie. "It's an animal with an hump on its back."

"Nonsense," said the Unwiseman. "A vocabulary is nothing of the sort. It's a—a sort of little bureau talkers have to keep their words in. It's a sort of word-cabinet. I haven't really got one, but that's because I don't need one. I have so few words I can carry them in my head, and if I can't, I

The Unwiseman drops words out of his vocabulary.

jot them down on a piece of paper. It's a splendid idea, that. It's helped me lots of times in conversation. I'm as fond of the word microcosm as I am of vocabulary, too, but I never can remember it, so I keep it on a piece of paper in my vest-pocket. Whenever I want to use it, I know just where to find it."

" And what does microcosm mean ?" asked Mollie.

"I don't know," said the Unwiseman; "but few people do; and if I use it, not one person in a thousand would dare take me up, so I just sprinkle it around to suit myself."

As the Unwiseman spoke, the postman came to the door with a letter.

"Ah!" said the Unwiseman, opening it and reading it. " I am sorry to say that I must leave you now. I have an engagement with my hatter this afternoon, and if I don't go now he will be much disappointed."

" Is that letter from him ?" asked Mollie.

" Oh no," said the Unwiseman, putting on his coat. " It is from myself. I thought about the engagement last night, and fearing that I might forget it I wrote a short note to myself reminding me of it. This is the note. Good-bye."

"Good-bye," said Mollie, and then, as the Unwiseman went off to meet his hatter, she and the others deemed it best to go home.

"But why did he say he expected you to call and then seemed surprised to see you?" asked the new doll.

"Oh—that's his way," said Mollie. "You'll get used to it in time."

But the new doll never did, for she was a proud wax-doll, and never learned to love the Unwiseman as I do for his sweet simplicity and never-ending good nature.

VIII

THE
UNWISEMAN
TURNS POET.
In which the Unwiseman
goes into
literature.

THE ground was white with snow when Mollie awakened from a night of pleasant dreams. The sun shone brightly, and as the little girl looked out of her bed-room window it seemed to her as if the world looked like a great wedding-cake, and she was very much inclined to go out of doors and cut a slice out of it and gobble it up, just as if it were a wedding-cake and not a world.

Whistlebinkie agreed with her that that was the thing to do, but there were music-lessons and a little reading to be done before

139

Mollie could hope to venture out, and as for Whistlebinkie, he was afraid to go out alone for fear of getting his whistle clogged up with snow. Consequently it was not until after luncheon that the two inseparable companions, accompanied by Mollie's new dog, Gyp, managed to get out of doors.

"Isn't it fine!" cried Mollie, as the snow crunched musically under her feet.

"Tsplendid!" whistled Whistlebinkie.

Gyp took a roll in the snow and gleefully barked to show that he too thought it wasn't half bad.

"I wonder what the Unwiseman is doing this morning," said Mollie, after they had romped about for some little while.

"I dare say he is throwing snow-balls at himself," said Whistlebinkie. "That's about as absurd a thing as any one can do, and he can always be counted upon to be doing things that haven't much sense to 'em."

"I've half a mind to go and see what he's doing," said Mollie.

"Let's," ejaculated Whistlebinkie, and Gyp indicated that he was ready for the call by rushing pell-mell over the snow-encrusted lawn in the direction of the spot where the Unwiseman's house had last stood.

"Gyp hasn't learned that the Unwiseman moves his house about every day," said Mollie.

"Dogs haven't much sense," observed Whistlebinkie, with a superior air. "It takes them a long time to learn things, and they can't whistle."

"That they haven't," came a voice from behind Whistlebinkie. "That little beast has destroyed eight lines of my poem with his horrid paws."

Mollie turned about quickly and there was the house of the Unwiseman, and sitting on the door-step was no less a person than the old gentleman himself, gazing ruefully at some rough, irregular lines which he had traced in the snow with a stick, and which were punctuated here and there by what were unmistakably the paw-marks of Gyp.

"Why—hullo!" said Mollie; "moved your house over here, have you?"

"Yes," replied the Unwiseman. "There is so much snow on the ground that I was afraid it would prevent your coming to see me if I let the house stay where it was, and I wanted to see you very much."

"It was very thoughtful of you," said Mollie.

"Yes; but I can't help that, you know," said the Unwiseman. "I've got to be thoughtful in my new business. Thoughts and snow and a stick are things I can't get along without, seeing that I haven't a slate or pen, ink and paper, in the house."

"You've got a new business, then, have you?" said Mollie.

"Yes," the Unwiseman answered. "I had

142

to have. When the Christmas toy business failed I cast about to find some other that would pay for my eclaires. My friend the hatter wanted me to go in with him, but when I found out what he wanted me to do I gave it up."

"What did he want you to do?" asked Mollie.

"Why, there is a restaurant next door to his place where two or three hundred men went to get their lunch every day," said the Unwiseman. "He wanted me to go in there and carelessly knock their hats off the pegs and step on them and spoil them, so that they'd have to call in at his shop and buy new ones. My salary was to be fifteen a week."

"Fifteen dollars?" whistled Whistlebinkie in amazement, for to him fifteen dollars was a princely sum.

"No," returned the Unwiseman. "Fifteen eclaires, and I was to do my own fighting with the ones whose hats were spoiled. That wouldn't pay, because before the end of the week I'd be in the hospital, and I am told that people in hospitals are not allowed to eat eclaires."

"And so you declined to go into that business?" asked Mollie.

"Exactly," returned the Unwiseman. "I felt very badly on my way back home, too. I had hoped that the hat- ter wanted to employ me as a demon- strator."

"A demonstrator."

"A what?" cried Whistlebinkie.

"A demonstrator," repeated the Unwiseman. "A demonstrator

144

is one who demonstrates—a sort of a show-
man. In the hat business he would be a
man who should put on new styles of hats
so as to show people how people looked
in them. I suggested that to the hatter,
but he said no, it wouldn't do. It would
make customers hopeless. They couldn't
hope to look as well in his hats as I would,
and so they wouldn't buy them; and as he
wasn't in the hat trade for pleasure, he didn't
feel that he could afford a demonstrator like
me."

"And what did you do then?" asked Mollie.

"I was so upset that I got on board of a
horse-car to ride home, forgetting that the
horse-cars all ran the other way and that I
hadn't five cents in my pocket. That came
out all right though. I didn't have to walk
any further," said the Unwiseman. "The
conductor was so mad when he found out
that I couldn't pay my fare that he turned

the car around and took me back to the
hatter's again, where I'd got on. It was a
great joke, but he never saw it."

And the Unwiseman roared with laughter
as he thought of the joke on the conductor,
and between you and me, I don't blame him.

"Well, I got home finally, and was just
about to throw myself down with my head
out of the window to weep when I had an
idea," continued the Unwiseman.

"With your head out of the window?"
echoed Mollie. "What on earth was that for?"

"So that my tears wouldn't fall on the
carpet, of course," returned the Unwiseman.
"What else? I always weep out of the
window. There isn't any use of my damp-
ening the house up and getting rheumatism
just because it happens to be easier to weep
indoors. When you're as old as I am, you
have to be careful how you expose yourself
to dampness. Rheumatism might be fun for
you, because you can stay home from school,

"I always weep out of the window."—Page 146.

and be petted while you have it, but for me it's a very serious matter. I had it so bad once I couldn't lean my elbow on the din-ner-table, and it spoiled all the pleasure of dining."

"Well—go on and tell us what your idea was," said Mollie, with difficulty repressing a smile. "Are you going to patent your scheme of weeping through a window?"

"No, indeed," said the Unwiseman. "I'm willing to let the world have the benefit of my discoveries, and, besides, patenting things costs money, and you have to send in a model of your invention. I can't afford to build a house and employ a man to cry through a window just to supply the govern-ment with a model. My idea was this. As my tears fell to the ground my ears and nose got very cold—almost froze, in fact. There was the scheme in a nutshell. Tears rhyme with ears, nose with froze. Why not write rhymes for the comic papers?"

"Oho!" said Mollie; "I see. You are going to be a poet."

"That's the idea," said the Unwiseman. "There's heaps of money in it. I know a man who gets a dollar a yard for writing poetry. If I can write ten yards of it a week I shall make eight dollars anyhow, and maybe ten. All shop-keepers calculate to have remnants of their stock left over, and I've allowed two yards out of every ten for remnants. The chief trouble I have is in finding writing materials. I haven't any pen and ink; I don't own any slates; the only paper I have in the house is the wall paper and a newspaper, and I can't use them, because the wall paper is covered with flowers and the newspaper is where I get my ideas— besides, it's all the library I've got. I didn't know what to do until this morning when I got up and found the ground all covered with snow. Then it came to me all of a sudden, why not get a stick and write your

poems on the snow, and then maybe, if you
have luck, you call sell them before the thaw.
I dressed hurriedly and hastened down-stairs,
moved the house up near yours, so that I'd
be near you and be sure to see you, feeling
confident that you could get your papa to
come out and see the poems and maybe buy
them for his paper. Before long I had written thirty yards of poetry, and just as I had
finished what I thought was a fair day's work,
up comes that horrid Gyp and prances the
whole thing into nothing."

"Dear me!" said Whistlebinkie. "That
was too bad."

"Wasn't it!" sighed the Unwiseman. "It
was such a beautifully long poem—and what's
more, it isn't easy work. It's almost as hard
as shoveling snow, only, of course, you get
better pay for it."

"You can rewrite it, can't you?" asked
Mollie, gazing sadly at the havoc Gyp had
wrought in the Unwiseman's work.

"I am afraid not," said the Unwiseman. "My disappointment has driven it quite out of my head. I can only remember the title."

"What did you call it?" asked Mollie.

"It was a simple little title," replied t h e Unwiseman. "It was called 'A Poem, by Me.'"

"A Poem, by Me."

"And what was it about?" asked Mollie.

"About six hundred verses," said the Unwiseman; "and not one of 'em has escaped that dog. Those that he hasn't spoiled with his paws he has wagged his tail on, and he

150

chose the best one of the lot to lie on his back and wiggle on. It's very discouraging."

"I'm very sorry," said Mollie; "and if you want me to I'll punish Gyp."

"What good would that do me?" queried the Unwiseman. "If chaining him up would restore even half the poem, I'd say go ahead and chain him up; but it won't. The poem's gone, and there's nothing left for me to do but go in the house and stick my head out of the window and cry."

"Perhaps you can write another poem," said Mollie.

"That's true—I hadn't thought of that," said the Unwiseman. "But I don't think I'd better to-day. I've lost more money by the destruction of that first poem than I can afford. If I should have another ruined to-day, I'd be bankrupt."

"Well, I'll tell you what I'll do," said Mollie. "I'll ask papa to let me give you a lead-pencil and a pad to write your next poem on. How will that do?"

"I should be very grateful," said the Unwiseman; "and if with these he could give me a few dozen ideas and a rhyming dictionary it would be a great help."

"I'll ask him," said Mollie. "I'll ask him right away, and I haven't any doubt that he'll say yes, because he always gives me things I want if they aren't harmful."

"Very well," said the Unwiseman. "And you may tell him for me, Miss Whistlebinkie, that I'll show him how grateful I am to him and to you for your kind assistance by letting him have the first thousand yards of poetry I write for his paper at fifty cents a yard, which is just half what I shall make other people pay for them."

And so Mollie and Whistlebinkie bade the Unwiseman good-by for the time being, and went home. As Mollie had predicted, her father was very glad to give her the pencil

and the pad and a rhyming dictionary ; but
as he had no ideas to spare at the moment

The Unwiseman becomes a poet.

he had to deny the little maid that part of the
request.

What the Unwiseman did with the pad
and the pencil and the dictionary I shall tell
you in the next chapter.

IX

THE POEMS OF THE UNWISEMAN.

In which Mollie listens to some remarkable verses.

FEW days after he had received the pencil and pad and rhyming dictionary from Mollie, the Unwiseman wrote to his little benefactress and asked her to visit him as soon as she could.

"I've written eight pounds of poetry," he said in his letter, "and I'd like to know what you think of some of it. I've given up the idea of selling it by the yard because it uses up so much paper, and I'm going to put it out at a dollar a pound. If you wouldn't mind, I'd like to have you tell your papa about this and ask him if he hasn't any heavier paper than the lot he sent me. If he could let me have a million sheets of paper twice as heavy as the other I could write a pound of sonnits in half the time, and could accordingly afford to give them to him a little cheaper for

"I've written eight pounds of poetry!"

use in his newspaper. I'd have been up to see you last night, but somehow or other my house got moved out to Illinois, which was too far away. It is back again in New York this morning, however, so that you won't find any trouble in getting him to see the poetry, and, by the way, while I think of it, I wish you'd ask your papa if Illinois rhymes with boy or boys. I want to write a poem about Illinois, but I don't know whether to begin it with

> " ' O, the boys,
> Of Illinois,
> They utterly upset my equipoise';
>
> " ' O, thou boy,
> Of Illinois !
> My peace of mind thou dust destroy.'

"You see, my dear, it is important to know at the start whether you are writing about one boy or several boys; and that rhyming dictionary you sent me doesn't say anything about such a contiguity. You might ask him, too, what is the meaning of contiguity. It's a word I admire, and I want to work it in somewhere where it will not only look well, but make a certain amount of sense.

> "Yoors tooly,
>
> "ME."

It was hardly to be expected, after an invi-

tation of this sort, that Mollie should delay
visiting the Unwiseman for an instant, so
summoning Whistlebinkie and Gyp, she and
her two little friends started out, and ere
long they caught sight of the Unwiseman's
house, standing on one corner of the village
square, and in front of it was a peculiar looking booth, something like a banana-stand in
its general outlines. This was covered from
top to bottom with placards, which filled
Mollie with uncontrollable mirth, when she
saw what was printed on them. Here is
what some of them said:

GO TO ME'S FOR POTERY.

This was the most prominent of the placards, and was nailed to the top of the booth.
On the right side of this was:

LISENSED TO SELL SONNITS ON THE PREMISSES.

Off to the left, printed in red crayon, the curious old man had tacked this :

> EPIKS WROTE WHILE
> YOU WEIGHT.

Besides these signs, on the counter of this little stand were arranged a dozen or more piles of manuscript, and behind each of these piles were short sticks holding up small cards marked "five cents an ounce," "ten cents a pound," and back of all a larger card, which read :

> SPESHUL DISSCOUNTS TO ALL
> COSTUMERS ORDERING
> BY THE TUN.

"This looks like business," said Whistle-binkie.

"Yes," said Mollie, with a laugh. "Like the peanut business."

Gyp said nothing for a moment, but after

sniffing it all over began to growl at a placard at the base of the stand on which was
drawn by the Unwiseman's unmistakable
hand the picture of two small dogs playing
together with a line to this effect:

DOGGERELL A SPESHIALITY.

As Mollie and Whistlebinkie were reading
these signs the door of the Unwiseman's
house was opened and the proprietor appeared. He smiled pleasantly when he saw
who his visitors were, although if Mollie had
been close enough to him to hear it she
might have noticed that he gave a little sigh.

"I didn't recognize you at first," he said;
"I thought you might be customers, and I
delayed coming out so that you wouldn't
think I was too anxious to sell my wares.
Of course, I am very anxious to sell 'em, but
it don't do to let the public know that. Let
'em understand that you are willing to sell

and they'll very likely buy; but if you come
tumbling out of your house pell-mell every
time anybody stops to see what you've got
they'll think maybe you aren't well off, and
they'll either beat you down or not buy at
all."

"Aren't you afraid of being robbed
though?" Mollie asked.

"Oh, I wouldn't mind being robbed," replied the Unwiseman. "It would be a good
thing for me if somebody would steal a
pound or two of my poems. That would
advertise my business. I can't afford to
advertise my business, but if I should be
robbed it would be news, and, of course, the
newspapers would be full of it. Your father
doesn't know of any kind-hearted burglar
who's temporarily out of work who'd be
willing to rob a poor man without charge
does he?"

"No," said Mollie, "I don't think papa
knows any burglars at all. We have literary

men, and editors, and men like that visiting the house all the time, but so far we haven't had any burglars."

"Well, I suppose I'll have to trust to luck for 'em," sighed the Unwiseman; "though it would be a great thing if an extra should come out with great

"The newspapers would be full of it."

big black headlines, and newsboys yelling 'em out all over the country, 'The Unwiseman's Potery Stand Visited by Burglars! Eight Pounds of Triolets Missing! The Police on the Track of the Plunderers!'"

162

The unwiseman reads his poem, "My wish and why I wished it."—Page 162.

"It would be a splendid advertisement," said Mollie. "But I'm afraid you'll be a long time getting it. Have you any poems to show me?"

"Yes," said the Unwiseman, running his eye over his stock. "Yes, indeed, I have. Here's one I like very much. Shall I read it to you?"

"Yes, if you will," said Mollie. "What is it about?"

"It's about three dozen to the pound, the way I weigh it," replied the Unwiseman. "It's called 'My Wish, and Why I Wish It.'"

"That's an awfully long name, isn't it?" said Mollie.

"Yes, but it makes the poem a little heavier," replied the old man. "I've made up a little for its length, too, by making the poem short. It's only a quartrain. Here's how it goes:

" I wish the sun would shine at night,
Instead of in the day, dear,
For that would make the evenings bright,
And day time would be shadier."

" Why, that isn't bad!" cried Mollie.

" No," returned the Unwiseman. " I didn't try to make it bad, though I could have if I'd wanted to. But there's a great thing about the thought in that poem, and if you'll only look into it you'll see how wonderful it is. It can be used over and over again without anybody's ever noticing that it's been used before. Here's another poem with just the same idea running through it :

" I wish the oceans all were dry,
And arid deserts were not land, dear,
If we could walk on oceans—My !
And sail on deserts, 'twould be handier."

" How is that the same idea?" asked Mollie, a little puzzled to catch the Unwiseman's point.

"Why, the whole notion is that you wish things were as they aren't, that's all; and when you consider how many things there are in the world that are as they are and aren't as they aren't, you get some notion as to how many poems you can make out of that one idea. For instance, children hate to go to bed at night, preferring to fall asleep on the library rug. So you might have this:

" *I wish that cribs were always rugs,*
　　'Twould fill me chock up with delight,
　For then, like birds and tumble-bugs,
　　I'd like to go to bed at night."

"Tumble-bugs don't like to go to bed at night," said Mollie. "They like to buzz around and hit their heads against the wall."

"I know that; but I have two excuses for using tumble-bugs in that rhyme. In the first place, I haven't written that rhyme yet, and so it can't be criticized. It's only what

the dictionary people would call extempori-
ous. I made it up on the spur of the moment, and from that standpoint it's rather
clever. The other excuse is that even if I
had written it as I spoke it, poets are allowed
to say things they don't exactly mean, as
long as in general they bring out their idea
clearly enough to give the reader something
to puzzle over."

"Well, I suppose you know what you
mean," said Mollie, more mystified than ever.
" Have you got any more poems?"

"Yes. Here's a new bit of Mother Goose
I've dashed off:

> " *Namby Pamby sat on the fence,*
> *Namby Pamby tumbled from thence.*
> *Half the queen's donkeys, her dog, and her cat,*
> *Could not restore Namby to where he was at."*

"Why!" cried Mollie. "You can't write
that. It's nothing but Humpty Dumpty all
over again."

"You're all wrong there," retorted the Unwiseman. "And I can prove it. You

"Could not restore Namby to where he was at."

say that I can't write that. Well, I *have*

written it, which proves that I *can*. As for its being Humpty Dumpty all over again, that's plain nonsense. Namby Pamby is not Humpty Dumpty. Namby Pamby begins with an N and a P, while Humpty Dumpty begins with H and D. Then, again, Humpty Dumpty sat on a wall. My hero sat on a fence. Humpty Dumpty fell. Namby Pamby tumbled—and so it goes all through the poem. Mine is entirely different. Besides, it's a hysterical episode, and I've got just as much right to make poems about hystery as Mother Goose had."

"Maybe you're right," said Mollie. "But if I were you, I wouldn't write things that are too much like what other people have written."

"I don't see why," said the Unwiseman, impatiently. "If Peter Smith writes a poem that everybody likes and buys, I want to write something as much like what Peter Smith has made a fortune out of as Peter

Smith has. That's the point. But we won't quarrel about it. Girls don't know much about business, and men do. I'm a man and you're only a girl."

"Well, I think Mollie's right," put in Whistlebinkie.

"You have to," retorted the Unwiseman. "If you didn't, she'd pack you up in a box and send you out to the sheathen."

"The what?" asked Mollie.

"The sheathen. Little girl savages. I call 'em sheathen to extinguish them from heathen, who are, as I understand it, little boy savages," explained the

"The Sheathen."

Unwiseman. "But what do you think of this for a poem. It's called Night, and you mustn't laugh at it because it is serious:

169

" Oh night, dear night, in street and park,
Where'er thou beest thou'rt always dark.
Thou dustent change, O sweet brunette,
No figgleness is thine, you bet.
And what I love the best, on land or sea,
Is absence of the vice of figglety."

"What's figglety?" asked Mollie.

"Figglety?" echoed the Unwiseman. "Don't you know that? Figglety is figgleness, or the art of being figgle."

"But I don't know what being figgle is," said Mollie.

"Hoh!" sneered the Unwiseman, angry at Mollie's failure to understand and to admire his serious poem. "Where have you been brought up? Figgle is changing. If you pretend to like pie to-day better than anything, and change around to pudding to-morrow, you are figgle. Some people spell it fickle, but somehow or other I like figgle better. It's a word of my own, figgle is, while fickle is a word everybody uses—but I

170

won't argue with you any more," he added with an impatient gesture. "You've found fault with almost everything I've done, and I'm not going to read any more to you. It's discouraging enough to have people pass you by and not buy your poems, without reading 'em to a little girl that finds fault with 'em, backed up in her opinion by a pug dog and a rubber doll like Whistlebinkie. Some time, when you are better natured, I'll read more to you, but now I won't."

Saying which, the Unwiseman turned away and walked into his house, banging the door behind him in a way which plainly showed that he was offended.

Mollie and Whistlebinkie and Gyp went silently home, very unhappy about the Unwiseman's temper, but, though they did not know it, they were very fortunate to get away before the Unwiseman discovered that the mischievous Gyp had chewed up three pounds of sonnets while their author was reading his poem " Night," so that on the whole, I think, they were to be congratulated that things turned out as they did.

X

THE UNWISEMAN'S LUNCHEON

In which the Unwiseman makes some sensible remarks on eating.

"WHISTLEBINKIE," said Mollie, one morning in the early spring, "it's been an awful long time since we saw the Unwiseman."

"Thasso," whistled Whistlebinkie. "I wonder what's become of him."

"I can't even guess," said Mollie. "I asked papa the other morning if he had seen any of his poetry in print and he said he hadn't so far as he knew, although he had read several books of poetry lately that

173

sounded as if he'd written them. I say we
go out and try to find him."

"Thasoots me," said Whistlebinkie.

"What's that?" said Mollie. "You still
talk through the top of your hat so much
that I really can't make out what you say
half the time."

"I forgot," said Whistlebinkie, meekly.
"What I meant to say was that that suits
me. I'd like very much to see him again
and hear some of his poetry."

"I don't much think he's stayed in that
business," observed Mollie. "He's had time
enough to be in sixteen different kinds of
businesses since we saw him, and I'm pretty
certain that he's tried eight of them any how."

"I guess may be so," said Whistlebinkie.
"He's a great tryer, that old Unwiseman."

Mollie donned her new spring hat and
Whistlebinkie treated his face and hands to
a dash of cold water, after which they started
out.

"It's the same old question now," said Mollie, as she stood on the street corner, wondering which way to turn. "Where would we better go to find him?"

"Well, it seems to me," said Whistlebinkie, after a moment's thought, "it seems to me that we'd better look for him in just the same place he was in the last time we saw him."

"I don't see why," returned Mollie. "We never did that before."

"That's why," explained Whistlebinkie. "He's such an unaccountable old man that he's sure to turn up where you least expected him. Now, as I look at it, the place where we least expect to find him is where he was before. Therefore I say let's go there."

"You're pretty wise after all, Whistlebinkie," said Mollie, with an approving nod. "We'll go there."

And it turned out that Whistlebinkie was right.

The house of the Unwiseman was found standing in precisely the same place in which they had last seen it, but pasted upon the front door was a small placard which read, "Gawn to Lunch. Will be Back in Eight Weeks."

"Dear me!" cried Whistlebinkie, as Mollie read the placard to him. "He must have

"He must be fearfully hungry to go to a lunch it will take that long to eat."

been fearfully hungry to go to a lunch it will take that long to eat."

Mollie laughed. "I guess maybe I know him well enough to know what that means," she said. "It means that he's inside the house and doesn't want to be bothered by anybody. Let's go round to the back door and see if that is open."

This was no sooner said than done, but the back door, like the first, was closed. Like the front door, too, it bore a placard, but this one read, "As I said before, I've gone to lunch. If you want to know when I'll be back, don't bother about ringing the bell to ask me, for I shall not answer. Go round to the front door and find out for yourself. Yours tooly, the Unwiseman. P. S. I've given up the potery business, so if you're a editor, I don't want to see you any how; but if your name's Mollie, knock on the kitchen window and I'll let you in."

"I thought so," said Mollie. "He's inside."

Then the little girl tiptoed softly up to the

kitchen window and peeped in, and there the old gentleman sat nibbling on a chocolate eclaire and looking as happy as could be.

Mollie tapped gently on the window, and the Unwiseman, hurriedly concealing his half-eaten eclaire in the folds of his newspaper, looked anxiously toward the window to see who it might be that had disturbed him. When he saw who it was his face wreathed with smiles, and rushing to the window he threw it wide open.

"Come right in," he cried. "I'm awfully glad to see you."

"I can't climb in this way," said Mollie. "Can't you open the door?"

"Can't possibly," said the Unwiseman. "Both doors are locked. I've lost the keys. You can't open doors without keys, you know. That's why I lost them. I'm safe from burglars now."

"But why don't you get new keys?" said Mollie.

"What's the use? I know where I lost the others, and when my eight weeks' absence is up I can find them again. New keys would only cost money, and I'm not so rich that I can spend money just for the fun of it," said the Unwiseman.

"Then, I suppose, I can't come in at all," said Mollie.

"Oh, yes, you can," said the Unwiseman. "Have you an Alpine stock?"

"What's that?" said Mollie.

"Ho!" jeered the Unwiseman. "What's an Alpine stock! Ha, ha! Not to know that; I thought little girls knew everything."

"Well, they do generally," said Mollie, resolved to stand up for her kind. "But I'm not like all little girls. There are some things I don't know."

"I guess there are," said the Unwiseman, with a superior air. "You don't know what rancour means, or fixity, or garrulousness."

179

"No, I don't," Mollie admitted. "What do they mean?"

"I'm not in the school-teacher business, and so I shan't tell you," said the Unwiseman, with a wave of his hand. "Besides, I really don't know myself—though I'm not a little girl. But I'll tell you one thing. An Alpine stock is a thing to climb Alps with, and a thing you can climb an Alp with ought to help you climbing into a kitchen window, because kitchen windows aren't so high as Alps, and they don't have snow on 'em in spring like Alps do."

"Oh," said Mollie. "That's it—is it? Well, I haven't got one, and I don't know where to get one, so I can't get in that way."

"Then there's only two things we can do," observed the Unwiseman. "Either I must send for a carpenter and have him build a new door or else I'll have to lend you a step-ladder. I guess, on the whole, the step-ladder is cheaper. It's certainly not so noisy as a carpenter. However, I'll let you choose. Which shall it be?"

"The step-ladder, I guess," said Mollie. "Have you got one?"

"No," returned the Unwiseman; "but I have a high-chair which is just as good. I always keep a high-chair in case some one should bring a baby here to dinner. I'd never ask any one to do that, but unexpected things are always happening, and I like to be prepared. Here it is."

Saying which the Unwiseman produced a high-chair and lowered it to the ground. Upon this Mollie and Whistlebinkie climbed up to the window-ledge, and were shortly comfortably seated inside this strange old man's residence.

"I see you've given up the poetry business," said Mollie, after a pause.

"Yes," said the Unwiseman. "I couldn't make it pay. Not that I couldn't sell all I could write, but that I couldn't write all that

181

I could sell. You see, people don't like to be disappointed, and I had to disappoint people all the time. I couldn't turn out all they wanted. Two magazine editors sent in orders for their winter poetry. Ten tons apiece they ordered, and I couldn't deliver more than two tons apiece to 'em. That made them mad, and they took their trade elsewhere—and so it went. I disappointed everybody, and finally I found myself writing poetry for my own amusement, and as it wasn't as amusing as some other things, I gave it up."

"But what ever induced you to put out that sign, saying that you wouldn't be back for eight weeks?" asked Mollie.

"I didn't say that," said the Unwiseman. "I said I *would* be back *in* eight weeks. I shall be. What I wanted was to be able to eat my lunch undisturbed. I've been eating it for five weeks now, and at the end of three weeks I shall be through."

182

"It musterbin a big lunch," said Whistle-binkie.

"I don't know any such word as muster-bin," said the Unwiseman, severely; "but as for the big lunch, it was big. One whole eclaire."

"I could eat an eclaire in five seconds," said Mollie.

"No doubt of it," retorted the Unwiseman. "So could I; but I know too much for that. I believe in getting all the enjoyment out of a thing that I can; and what's the sense of gobbling all the pleasure out of an eclaire in five seconds when you can spread it over eight weeks? That's a queer thing about you wise people that I can't understand. When you have something pleasant on hand you go scurrying through it as though you were afraid somebody was going to take it away from you. You don't make things last as you should ought to."

"Excuse me," interrupted Whistlebinkie,

who had been criticized so often about the way he spoke, that he was resolved to get even. "Is 'should ought to' a nice way to speak?"

"It's nice enough for me," retorted the Unwiseman. "And as this is my house I have a right to choose the language I speak here. If you want to speak some other language, you can go outside and speak it."

Poor Whistlebinkie squeaked out an apology and subsided.

"Take bananas, for instance," said the Unwiseman, not deigning to notice Whistlebinkie's apology. "I dare say if your mother gives you a banana, you go off into a corner and gobble it right up. Now I find that a nibble tastes just as good as a bite, and by nibbling you can get so many more tastes out of that banana, as nibbles are smaller than bites, and instead of a banana lasting a week, or two weeks or eight weeks, it's all gone in ten seconds. You might do the

184

" If you want to speak some other language, you can go outside and speak it."
—Page 184.

same thing at the circus and be as sensible
as you are when you gobble your banana.
If the clown cracked his jokes and the trape-
zuarius trapozed, and the elephants danced,
and the bare-back riders rode their horses all
at once,
you'd have
just as much
circus as you get
the way you do
it now, only it
wouldn't be so
pleasant. Pleas-
ure, after all, is
like butter, and
it ought to be
spread. You

" Pleasure ought to be spread."

wouldn't think of eating a whole pat of butter
at one gulp, so why should you be greedy
about your pleasure ?"

"Thassounds very sensible," put in Whistlebinkie.

185

"It is sensible," said the Unwiseman, with a kindly smile; "and that is why, having but one eclaire, I make it last me eight weeks. There isn't any use of living like a prince for five minutes and then starving to death for seven weeks, six days, twenty-three hours, and fifty-five minutes."

Here the Unwiseman opened the drawer of his table and took out the eclaire to show it to Mollie.

"It doesn't look very good," said Mollie.

"That's true," said the Unwiseman; "but that helps. It's awfully hard work the first day to keep from nibbling it up too fast, but the second day it's easier, and so it goes all along until you get to the fourth week, and then you don't mind only taking a nibble. If it stayed good all the while, I don't believe I could make it last as long as I want to. So you see everything works for good under my system of luncheoning. In the first place, the pleasure of a thing lasts a long time; in the second, you learn to resist temptation ; in the third place, you avoid greediness ; and last of all, after a while you don't mind not be-ing greedy."

With this the old gen-tleman put the eclaire away, locked the drawer, and began to tell Mollie and Whistlebinkie all about the new business he was going into.

"The old gentleman put the eclaire away."

XI

THE UNWISEMAN'S NEW BUSINESS

In which the Old Gentleman and Mollie and Whistlebinkie start on their travels.

I have at last found something to do," he said, as he locked the eclaire up in the drawer, "which will provide me in my old age with all the eclaires I need, with possibly one or two left over for my friends."

"Thassnice," whistled Whistlebinkie.

"Yes," said the Unwiseman. "It's very nice, particularly if you are one of my friends, and come in for your share of the

189

left-over eclaires—as, of course, you and Mollie will do. It all grew out of my potery business, too. You see, I didn't find that people who wanted potery ever bought it from a street-corner stand, but from regular potery peddlers, who go around to the newspaper offices and magazines with it, done up in a small hand-bag. So I gave up the stand and made a small snatchel——"

"A small what?" demanded Mollie.

"A small snatchel," repeated the Unwiseman. "A snatchel is a bag with a handle to it."

"Oh—I know. You mean a satchel," said Mollie.

"Maybe I do," observed the Unwiseman. "But I thought the word was snatchel, because it was a thing you could snatch up hurriedly and run to catch a train with. Anyhow, I made one and put some four or five pounds of potery in it, and started out to sell it. The first place I went to they said they liked my potery very much, but they couldn't use it because it didn't advertise anything. They wanted sonnets about the best kind of soap that ever was; or what they called a hook-and-eye lyric; or perhaps a few quatrains about baking-powders, or tooth-wash, or some kind of silver-polish. People don't read poems about mysteries and little red school-houses, and patriotism any more, they said; but if a real poet should write about a new kind of a clothes-wringer or a patent pickle he'd make a fortune, be-cause he'd get his work published on fences and in railroad cars, which everybody sees, instead of in magazines that nobody reads."

"I've seen lots of those kinds of poems," said Mollie.

"They're mighty good reading, too," said Whistlebinkie. "And is that what you are going to do?"

"Not I!" retorted the Unwiseman, scorn-fully. "No, indeed, I'm not. Shakespeare never did such a thing, and I don't believe Milton did either, and certainly I shall not try it. The next place I went to they said they liked my potery well enough to print it,

but I'd have to pay for having it done, which was very hard, because I hadn't any money. The next place they took a sonnet and said they'd pay

"They'd pay for it when they published it."

for it when they published it, and when I asked when that would be, they said in about thirty-seven years."

"Mercy!" cried Mollie.

"That's what I said," said the Unwiseman, ruefully. "So again I went on until I found an editor who was a lovely man. He read all my things through, and when he'd finished he said he judged from the quality of my potery I must be a splendid writer of prose."

192

Whistlebinkie laughed softly.

"Yes," said the Unwiseman, "that's what he said. 'Mr. Unwiseman,' said he, 'after reading your poetry, it seems to me your *forte* is prose.' And I told him perhaps he was right, though I didn't know what he meant. At any rate, he was very good to me, and asked me where I lived, and all that. When I told him that I lived everywhere; how I just moved my house around to suit myself, and lived one day here and another day in Illinois, and another in Kamschatka, he grew interested at once."

"I should think he might," put in Mollie. "I didn't know you could move as far as Kamschatka."

"Certainly I can," said the Unwiseman; "and in a way that is what I am going to do. I have been engaged to travel in various parts of the world just by moving my house around at will, and what I see and do under

193

such circumstances I am to write up for that editor's paper."

"Why it's perfectly splendid!" cried Mollie, clapping her hands together with glee at the very idea. "I wish I could go with you."

"Me too!" whistled Whistlebinkie.

"Woof—woof!" barked Gyp, which the Unwiseman took to mean that Gyp wished also to be included.

"All right," said the Unwiseman. "I've no objection."

"I don't know what they'd say at home," said Mollie, as she thought of possible objections to the trip.

"Why they won't say anything," said the Unwiseman. "I'll only travel afternoons. We'll be back every day by six o'clock, and I don't suppose we'll start much before three. This house is a rapid traveller once she gets started. Just wait a minute and I'll show you. Sit tight in your chairs now. One—two—three—LET HER GO!"

The old gentleman touched a button in the wall. The house shook violently for a second, apparently whizzed r a p i d l y through the air, if the whistling of the wind outside meant any- thing, and then sud- denly, with a thump and a bump, came to a standstill.

"Here we are," said the Unwiseman, opening the door. "Come outside."

The little party emerged, and Mol- lie was amazed to find herself standing on the top of a won-

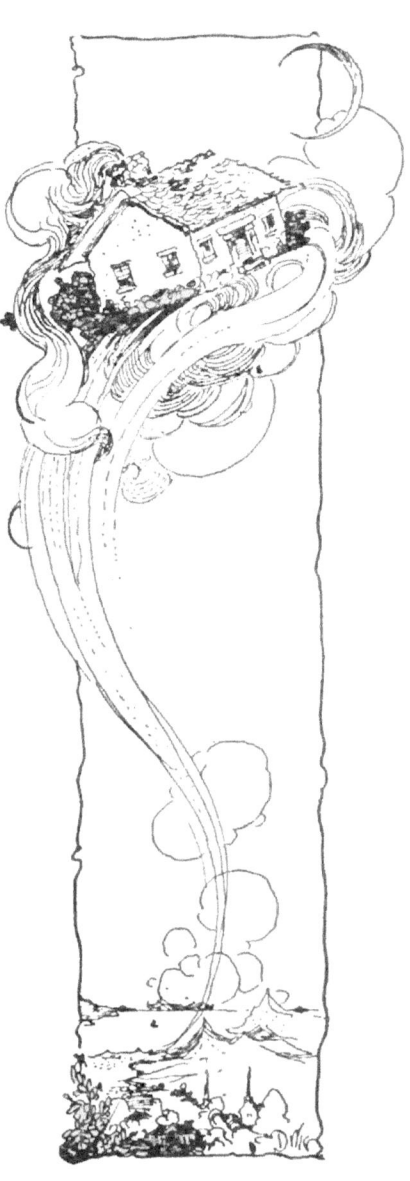

"The house whizzed rapidly through the air."

derful hill gazing out over the waters of a beautiful body of water of the most heavenly blue. At her feet a little yellowish city nestled into the hillside, and across a strip of silvery water was a huge and frowning fortress.

"This, Miss Whistlebinkie, is the city of Havana," said the Unwiseman to the astonished little maid. "You have come all the way from home to Cuba in five seconds—a distance of 1200 miles. So you see we can do all our travelling in the afternoons, and without your being away from your home any more than you naturally are during your play-time hours."

Mollie made no answer for a moment. She was too astonished to speak. Whistlebinkie was the first to recover, and he was not long in expressing his sentiments.

"Imagoin'," he whistled.

Gyp barked a similar resolution, whereupon Mollie said she'd see.

"But let us hurry back home again," she added, somewhat anxiously. She did not quite like being so far away from home without her mother knowing it.

"Certainly," said the Unwiseman, touching the button again. The violent shaking and whizzing sounds were repeated, and again, with a thump and a bump, the house came to a standstill. The Unwiseman opened the front door, and there they were, safe and sound, in the back yard of Mollie's home.

That night the little girl told the story of the day's adventure to her father, and he said that, under the circumstances, he had not the slightest objection to her making the grand tour of the world.

"Only," he said, "you must remember, dear, to be home to supper. Even if you find yourself at the coronation of a king, remember that it is your duty to be punctual at your meals. London, Paris, Pekin, or Kalamazoo are always ready to be seen,

197

night or day, no matter what the time, but breakfast, dinner, and supper do not go on forever, and are served only at stated hours."

And so Mollie and Gyp and Whistlebinkie joined in the adventures of the UNWISEMAN ABROAD, and, in point of fact, they started off that very afternoon, though what they saw I do not know, for I have not encountered them since. I only know that their journey was safely accomplished, and that they all got home that night without harm, for Mollie's papa told me so. He also told me, in confidence, that I might hope soon to hear some remarkable tales on the subject of their adventures; and if I do, I shall not fail to let you in turn hear what happened to "MOLLIE AND THE UNWISEMAN ABROAD."

www.ingramcontent.com/pod-product-compliance
Lightning Source LLC
Chambersburg PA
CBHW051648260626
47170CB00004B/1398